BROKEN

John Blackburn was born in 1923 in the
second son of a clergyman. Blackburn started attending Haileybury College near London in 1937, but his education was interrupted by the onset of World War II; the shadow of the war, and that of Nazi Germany, would later play a role in many of his works. He served as a radio officer during the war in the Mercantile Marine from 1942 to 1945, and resumed his education afterwards at Durham University, earning his bachelor's degree in 1949. Blackburn taught for several years after that, first in London and then in Berlin, and married Joan Mary Clift in 1950. Returning to London in 1952, he took over the management of Red Lion Books.

It was there that Blackburn began writing, and the immediate success in 1958 of his first novel, *A Scent of New-Mown Hay*, led him to take up a career as a writer full time. He and his wife also maintained an antiquarian bookstore, a secondary career that would inform some of Blackburn's work, including the bibliomystery *Blue Octavo* (1963). *A Scent of New-Mown Hay* typified the approach that would come to characterize Blackburn's twenty-eight novels, which defied easy categorization in their unique and compelling mixture of the genres of science fiction, horror, mystery, and thriller. Many of Blackburn's best novels came in the late 1960s and early 1970s, with a string of successes that included the classics *A Ring of Roses* (1965), *Children of the Night* (1966), *Nothing but the Night* (1968; adapted for a 1973 film starring Christopher Lee and Peter Cushing), *Devil Daddy* (1972) and *Our Lady of Pain* (1974). Somewhat unusually for a popular horror writer, Blackburn's novels were not only successful with the reading public but also won widespread critical acclaim: the *Times Literary Supplement* declared him 'today's master of horror' and compared him with the Grimm Brothers, while the *Penguin Encyclopedia of Horror and the Supernatural* regarded him as 'certainly the best British novelist in his field' and the *St. James Guide to Crime & Mystery Writers* called him 'one of England's best practicing novelists in the tradition of the thriller novel'.

By the time Blackburn published his final novel in 1985, much of his work was already out of print, an inexplicable neglect that largely continued until Valancourt began republishing his novels in 2013. John Blackburn died in 1993.

Greg Gbur is an associate professor of physics and optical science at the University of North Carolina at Charlotte. He writes the long-running blog 'Skulls in the Stars', which discusses classic horror fiction, physics and the history of science, as well as the curious intersections between the three topics. His science writing has recently been featured in 'The Best Science Writing Online 2012,' published by Scientific American. He has introduced four other John Blackburn titles for Valancourt Books.

By John Blackburn

A Scent of New-Mown Hay (1958)*
A Sour Apple Tree (1958)
Broken Boy (1959)*
Dead Man Running (1960)
The Gaunt Woman (1962)
Blue Octavo (1963)*
Colonel Bogus (1964)
The Winds of Midnight (1964)
A Ring of Roses (1965)
Children of the Night (1966)
The Flame and the Wind (1967)*
Nothing but the Night (1968)*
The Young Man from Lima (1968)
Bury Him Darkly (1969)*
Blow the House Down (1970)
The Household Traitors (1971)*
Devil Daddy (1972)
For Fear of Little Men (1972)
Deep Among the Dead Men (1973)
Our Lady of Pain (1974)*
Mister Brown's Bodies (1975)
The Face of the Lion (1976)*
The Cyclops Goblet (1977)*
Dead Man's Handle (1978)
The Sins of the Father (1979)
A Beastly Business (1982)*
The Book of the Dead (1984)
The Bad Penny (1985)*

* Available or forthcoming from Valancourt Books

JOHN BLACKBURN

BROKEN BOY

With a new introduction by

GREG GBUR

VALANCOURT BOOKS

Broken Boy by John Blackburn
First published London: Secker and Warburg, 1959
First Valancourt Books edition 2013
NOTE: This edition is reprinted from the first U.S. edition, published by Mill & Morrow in 1962.

Published by Valancourt Books, Kansas City, Missouri
Publisher & Editor: JAMES D. JENKINS
20th Century Series Editor: SIMON STERN, University of Toronto
http://www.valancourtbooks.com

Library of Congress Cataloging-in-Publication Data

Blackburn, John, 1923-
Broken boy / by John Blackburn ; with a new introduction by Greg Gbur. – First Valancourt Books edition.
p. cm.
ISBN 978-1-939140-14-2 (*acid free paper*)
1. Police – England – Fiction. 2. Murder – Investigation – England – Fiction. 3. Mystery fiction. I. Title.
PR6052.L34B76 2013
823'.914–dc23

2013003253

All Valancourt Books publications are printed on acid free paper that meets all ANSI standards for archival quality paper.

Also available as an electronic book.
Set in Dante MT 11/14

INTRODUCTION

THERE are typically two reactions that a reader will have in coming to the climax of a John Blackburn novel: "Aha!" or "Whoa!" The "Aha!" comes from the unraveling of an incredibly baffling mystery of the sort that Blackburn was a master at weaving; the "Whoa!" comes from learning exactly how diabolical the underlying idea of the story truly is. In the case of Blackburn's 1959 novel *Broken Boy*, both exclamations will likely arise.

John Fenwick Blackburn was born in 1923 in the village of Corbridge, England, the second son of a clergyman. He started attending Haileybury College near London in 1937, but his education was interrupted by the onset of World War II; the shadow of the war, and that of Nazi Germany, would later play a role in many of his works. He served as a radio officer during the war in the Mercantile Marine from 1942 to 1945, and resumed his education afterwards at Durham University, earning his bachelor's degree in 1949. Blackburn taught for several years after that, first in London and then in Berlin, and married Joan Mary Clift in 1950. Returning to London in 1952, he took over the management of Red Lion Books.

It was there that Blackburn began writing, and the immediate success in 1958 of his first novel, *A Scent of New-Mown Hay*, led him to take up a career as a writer full-time. He and his wife also maintained an antiquarian bookstore, a secondary career that would inform some of Blackburn's later work. A prolific author, Blackburn would write twenty-eight novels between 1958 and 1985; most of these were horror and thrillers, but his output also included one historical novel set in Roman times, *The Flame and the Wind* (1967).

Broken Boy was Blackburn's third novel, and represents a departure from his first two and their decidedly apocalyptic storylines. Whereas *A Scent of New-Mown Hay* and *A Sour Apple Tree* featured an unstoppable worldwide pandemic and a rapidly spreading plague of murder-suicides, respectively, *Broken Boy* involves a less global—though equally diabolical—threat. It begins as a classic "locked room" mystery: a woman is found murdered and drowned, and eyewitness testimony of her last moments leaves seemingly no possibility for the murder to have been committed. What follows is a well-crafted murder mystery, with a bevy of eccentric characters, sinister suspects, red herrings, perilous situations, and a surprising revelation at the end. As is Blackburn's style, the revelation is far more shocking and nasty than what is found in more conventional thrillers.

In fact, the novel is as much a horror story as a thriller, and Blackburn was well-known for blurring the line between the two genres. For the horror aspect of *Broken Boy*, Blackburn draws on what may be considered a long British tradition of introducing a conspiracy of "others" from outside who threaten to erode the fabric of society from within. Decades earlier, for instance, the author Richard Marsh featured sinister foreigners with supernatural powers in his 1897 novel *The Beetle* and his 1901 novel *The Joss* (both of which have been reprinted by Valancourt Books). Sax Rohmer stirred up fears of the "Yellow Peril" with his series of novels about the Chinese criminal mastermind Fu-Manchu, starting with *The Mystery of Fu-Manchu* in 1913. With its history as a major colonial power, the United Kingdom has long been a destination for immigrants from around the globe, especially from India. The surge of immigration, which really took off in the mid-19th century, created inevitable tension that served as natural fodder for writers seeking to scare and thrill their readers.

After World War II, however, the nature of immigration changed, with many refugees coming from countries that had been absorbed by the Soviet Union. The threat to society became less about race and culture and more about ideology, with fears of communist infiltration increasing as the Cold War heated up. These fears were also a natural inspiration for horror authors: it has been suggested that Jack Finney's 1955 novel *The Body Snatchers*, featuring alien spores that replace people with inhuman copies, is an allegory for the threat of communism. Blackburn's *Broken Boy* also features a danger that may be interpreted as an ideological one, but true to his style the ideology ends up being nastier than simple communism. In fact, the Soviet Union regularly plays an ambiguous role in many of Blackburn's novels, working as an ally as often as it serves as an enemy.

Nevertheless, the possibility of communist activity is what draws the interest of General Kirk, the protagonist of *Broken Boy.* When the woman murdered in the beginning of the novel is identified as Gerda Raine, a former East German spy who defected to the West, the crime is considered a potential national security issue. General Kirk, the head of the British Foreign Intelligence Office, takes over the investigation personally. Helping him are his assistant, Michael Howard, and Howard's girlfriend Penelope (Penny) Wise. All three share in the investigation, and all three wind up in great danger as a result of their inquiry.

Blackburn is well known for his use of recurring characters in his stories. The aging, jaded, yet brilliant General Kirk appeared in both of Blackburn's earlier novels, *A Scent of New-Mown Hay* and *A Sour Apple Tree*. His character combines a sharp deductive mind with world-weary cynicism, giving him aspects reminiscent of both Sherlock Holmes and James Bond. His experience in hunting Nazis at the end of the Second World War is shown to be a great asset in tracking down the various existential threats to the United Kingdom. Kirk's encyclopedic knowledge of politics and history serves him particularly well in solving the mystery of the Broken Boy, and he would go on to appear in a number of later Blackburn novels.

Penny Wise was first introduced in *A Sour Apple Tree* as the sister of a long-lost Nazi collaborator of British descent. A fiercely independent woman and skilled car mechanic, she aids Michael Howard in the search for her brother and the two fall in love in the process. By the start of *Broken Boy*, they are in a serious relationship but have not yet committed to marriage.

It is rather unusual for a series of horror novels to have a cast of recurring characters; in Blackburn's work, however, it could really be said that the main character is the diabolical idea behind the story itself. In each of Blackburn's novels, one can almost always identify a single ingenious idea that forms the core of the plot; Blackburn then weaves around this idea a wonderful tapestry of atmosphere, twists, and misdirection. This is reminiscent of another masterful author, Ray Bradbury, whose short stories are often based on a very simple concept. Unlike Bradbury, however, Blackburn's ideas are well-hidden and usually only revealed near the end of the tale; part of the fun in reading his novels is trying to figure out exactly what form that idea will take.

Critical reception of *Broken Boy* is surprisingly hard to pin down in newspaper archives; however, those reviews that can be found are uniformly positive. The May 6, 1962 edition of *The Times-Picayune* in New Orleans carries the short description, "A distinctly off-beat story dealing with devil-worshipping . . . Non-realistic, but with its share of suspense." A review in the April 22, 1962 edition of *The Ada Evening News* in Oklahoma is much less reserved in its praise, and is titled, "Hitchcock should take heed of fast-paced suspense tale." Its author says, "This is a bit of a Hitchcockian affair. A real 'chiller' as General Kirk, a secret service agent, unravels a mystery which is covered up with all sorts of good clues and yet baffles everyone . . . The book moves rapidly from beginning to end and Hitchcock ought to be advised. It would make a heck of a movie."

The same praise could be said of most of Blackburn's stories: they are captivating and intriguing from start to finish, and seem perfectly suited to film adaptation. Sadly, only two of Blackburn's novels have ever been adapted: *Nothing But the Night* was made into a film of the same name in 1973, and *The Gaunt Woman* was made into the television movie *Destiny of a Spy* in 1969.

Hopefully these new releases of John Blackburn's works will draw new attention to this neglected master of thrillers, horror, and unclassifiable tales that lie in between.

It is impossible to talk about the details of *Broken Boy*'s plot without spoiling it. However, it is also impossible *not* to talk about the central idea behind it! After the break I say a few words about the history behind *Broken Boy*; those wishing to experience the mystery of the novel should come back after reading it first.

* * *

The country of Madagascar, off the Eastern coast of Africa, is known to most people these days as a literal island of biodiversity, containing many unique species of animals that appear nowhere else in the world, such as the charming and iconic lemurs. What most people do not know, however (and I include myself among this number until reading *Broken Boy*), is that the island was ruled in the 19th century by a bloody and tyrannical queen who caused the deaths of hundreds of thousands of her subjects.

Princess Ramavo, the girl who would become Queen Ranavalona I, was born into nobility in 1778, and at first seemed destined to be a minor figure in Madagascar history. When she was young, however, her father became aware of a coup plot against the king and dutifully reported it. The coup was put down and as a reward Ramavo was betrothed to the king's heir, Prince Radama. However, tensions became strained between the heir prince and his wife, in part due to her failure to provide him a son of his own and in part due to his execution of a number of Ramavo's relatives to secure his own succession to the throne.

Radama I took the crown in 1810 at the age of 17 but died in 1828, possibly poisoned by his own wife. With no direct heir, the kingship was supposed to pass to the son of Radama's sister but, in the confused days following the death, Ramavo secured the support of military officials, judges and religious leaders, giving her the backing she needed to seize power. She immediately sought out and killed all of her political rivals, including the true successor to the throne, and was crowned Queen Ranavalona in August 1829.

The new queen resented the growing European influence in her nation, and quickly initiated a policy of isolationism and autarky (self-sufficiency). This enraged the French, who led an unsuccessful invasion of the nation in 1829. The attack underscored Madagascar's vulnerability, as it had lost access to modern weaponry when it severed ties with Europe. Fortunately for Ranavalona, a Frenchman named Jean Laborde (given a genuinely demonic role in *Broken Boy*) ended up shipwrecked off the coast of the island in 1832, and he possessed the engineering know-how to produce gunpowder, muskets and cannons. The queen gave him the resources and manpower to build and operate weapons factories, allowing her not only to secure her own borders but expand them by dominating neighboring kingdoms.

Ranavalona expanded her territory with remarkable ruthlessness. A policy of fanompoana—forced labor in lieu of tax payments—allowed her to maintain a large standing army. Many were lost in battle invading weaker lands, but much greater numbers were lost to malaria while stationed in the mosquito-infested lowlands. Resistance to her rule was met with mass executions and forced slavery. A scorched earth policy in conquered territories led to mass starvation.

Ranavalona also maintained the religious traditions of her country through violence and fear. Christianity was formally outlawed in 1835, and practitioners could be subject to fines, imprisonment, death by torture, or the traditional "trial by ordeal" known as *tangena*. Christians, or indeed any charged with a crime, could be tested by tangena, in which the poison of the tangena shrub would be fed to the accused along with three pieces of chicken skin. If the accused vomited up all three pieces of skin, he or she was innocent; a failure to do so indicated guilt and likely a horrible death.

All told, the combined effects of Ranavalona's rule are said to have reduced the population of the country from 5 million people to 2.5 million, a horrifying legacy and one that presents an ominous background for Blackburn's *Broken Boy*. But what of the cult of "Broken Boy" itself, as described by Blackburn? The queen's first chief adviser, Major-General Andriamihaja, was also her consort, and she had a son by him, Prince Rakoto. A family connection did not help Andriamihaja's prospects, however: in 1830 the queen signed his execution order, apparently persuaded to do so by her other advisers while she was drunk. Now an only parent to the young Rakoto, Ranavalona fought hard to keep her son (eventually to become King Radama II) as the heir to the throne against the schemes of the court. He claimed it in 1861, after the natural death of his mother, but his rule did not last long. His attempts at reform were unpopular amongst the ruling class, and in 1863 he was strangled in the palace by members of the military. Curiously, it is rumored that he survived the assassination attempt and lived out his life in anonymity in the north.

This history—a strong queen dominating and advocating for a weak and submissive son—forms the basis of the fictional cult of the Broken Boy. The idol itself was likely inspired by the traditional royal talismans of the Madagascar people, known as sampy. These idols or amulets supposedly conveyed powers or protections to the community that held them, and some came in crudely fashioned humanoid form. The greatest of these was Kelimalaza, which has been described* as "simply a small piece of wood resembling an insect, wrapped in scarlet cloth, and decorated in chains." The keepers of these talismans were accorded extensive respect and political power, but this came to an end when they attempted to exert this power over Queen Ranavalona II, a convert to Christianity, in 1869. The queen ordered the destruction of all sampy, and they were consigned to the fire, bringing at least an official end to the old ways in Madagascar.

At around the same time that tribal superstition was being crushed in Madagascar, another nation off of the African coast was experiencing its own growth in witchcraft—and Blackburn tied the two together in *Broken Boy*. By the late 1800s, articles appeared in popular British magazines about the cult of "Le Petit Albert" on the island of Mauritius, and murders and supernatural actions connected with it. Though by that time a British colony, Mauritius had earlier been under the control of the French for 100 years starting in 1710—and French travelers brought some of their own grimoires—books of magic—to the island.

Le Grand Albert and *Le Petit Albert* were two grimoires published in France in the mid-1600s. The former supposedly gets its name from the 13th century monk Albert Le Grand, though it is in fact a hodge-podge of information from a variety of old and modern

* Richard Lovett, *The History of the London Missionary Society, 1795-1895* (H. Frowde, 1899, Vol. 1), p. 734.

sources. Both *Le Grand* and *Le Petit* are books of "natural magic," combining traditional medicinal recipes with supernatural talismans, and both became immensely popular among the general public. The "wisdom" of *Le Petit Albert* made its way to the colony of Mauritius, where the native inhabitants took to its wisdom with deadly sincerity, as an 1884 article in *The Saturday Review* suggests:*

"One Picot, a black student of Le Petit Albert (the popular work of divination and magic), was accused of having killed and mutilated a child for purposes of the dark art. He was tried by our authorities, found guilty, and condemned to death. Picot, however [. . .] coolly told his judges that 'they could not hang him.' Nor did they. The house of the Chief Judge was instantly haunted by spirits who threw stones. Night after night showers of stones rattled about the slates."

From the story of Queen Ranavalona I and the traditions of Madagascar we can see most of the elements that Blackburn fashioned into a sinister cult threatening British society. He added to the threat by connecting it to a "genuine" outbreak of witchcraft in nearby Mauritius. This truly unique background—which to my knowledge has never been used as the basis of another horror story—demonstrates how John Blackburn's vast historical knowledge and fertile imagination could be combined to tell a gripping tale.

GREG GBUR

January 20, 2013

* "Witches in Mauritius," *The Saturday Review of Politics, Literature, Science, Art, and Finance*, volume 58 (1884), pp. 167-168.

BROKEN BOY

CHAPTER ONE

BECAUSE it was summer, nobody considered the motive of the birds. They came inland in strict formation and they seemed to know exactly where they were going. They crossed the light-house and the twin piers and the moored fishing fleet and turned West over the ship yards and the factories, where the town begins and the river has cut through rock into coal-seams and runs grey because there is not enough tide or current to cleanse it.

Black Back and Black Cap and Herring Gull they flew on and nobody thought why; for it was August and their wings were white and the sun was shining on the grey river and the dark buildings and the big smoky town looked almost pleasant in the sun.

They came down under the last of the bridges to a little back-water on the north bank of the river and the people on the bridge smiled at the pretty white pattern they made on its surface. Then a man of no importance leaned over a rail and threw a slice of bread from his lunch-basket towards them. It curved down, twisting as it fell, and landed in the center of the gulls. They rose, tearing up and away from it and for a moment the water was clear again. Then at the end of the bridge a woman started to scream; and into the city came the Broken Boy.

They pulled the body out with hooks and ropes and it looked very small and pathetic in its stained finery. They laid it on a sheet with its few possessions beside it and they stationed a guard on the back-water where it had floated. Then they took it away and washed it and sent for the experts.

Inspector Ellis had a long, successful career behind him and a reputation for hardness. He felt as cold as the girl as he looked at her body.

"Well, Doctor," he said, "what happened to her? I suppose most of those injuries came after death while she was floating."

Dr. Newcombe didn't answer him at once. He got up and pulled a cover over the trolley. Then he handed his gloves to an assistant.

"No, you're wrong, old boy," he said. "Quite wrong. The injuries that she received from the current and the birds are purely superficial. All of them are. Everything that really mattered was done on or about the time of death."

"But, but—she's been practically torn to pieces."

"Aye, Inspector Ellis, she has that. To be exact, she has received nine wounds from a longish knife. About a foot long I shouldn't wonder. At least five of those wounds would have proved fatal. Following that her face was beaten in with the usual, blunt, heavy instrument." He crossed to a wash-basin in the corner of the room and turned on the taps.

"Any idea who she was yet?"

"Perhaps, though we can't be sure at this stage. The boys found a diary in her bag with a name in it; Gladys Reeves. Could be hers I suppose, though there's nothing else to help us. No other writing at all. Only one other thing that might say something. Very curious ring on her finger. Plain gold, shaped like a pair of snakes entwined together. Initials inside. H.R. to G.R. We're checking on it now. No, at the moment we've no real idea who she was, though there's not the slightest doubt as to what she was."

"*What* she was. Just how do you mean?" Newcombe looked up sharply as he began to dry his hands. They were very strong, white hands and they had little gold freckles on their backs.

"She was a tart; listen to what they found on her." He reached in his pocket and pulled out a note book. "Yes, here we are. 'Apart from the diary, the following were found in the hand-bag of the deceased. A purse containing five one pound notes and six shillings in silver, one comb, one mirror which was probably broken during the struggle and a cellophane folder holding powder, rouge and lipstick.' Now we go on. 'In the back pocket of the bag we found a tube containing three contraceptives and six indecent photographs in an envelope.' Good enough for you, Doctor?" He pushed the book back into his pocket and his eyes were suddenly very weary.

"Yes, I'm afraid it's just the old nasty story. A young girl who starts out on that way of life and probably thinks she is doing quite well out of it. Then one fine day she runs into somebody who is different. Somebody who is quite disinterested in normal pursuits. The very worst kind of murderer we can get because we never have any rational link or motive to go on. And always—practically always, he is not satisfied with just one victim."

"I see, so you think that's the way it was." Newcombe took his coat from a hook and pulled out a crumpled packet of cigarettes. "Got a light on you?"

"Of course," Ellis struck a match and held it out to him. "Just what do you mean. It looks quite obvious doesn't it?"

"Oh, yes, it looks quite obvious. Far too obvious in fact. Thank you." He drew on his cigarette, inhaling deeply while his eyes flicked over to the shape on the trolley.

"You know, old man, there's something wrong here, something very, very wrong. You've been kind enough to tell me what you found on her, let me tell you what I found about her.

"This girl was aged between twenty and twenty-four and she had recently been ill. As far as I can make out she had been in the river for about fourteen hours before they brought her here. She had been almost cut to pieces with a knife and her face had been battered in after death. That might mean that her killer was a sex maniac but it might not. You see there was no sign of any sexual assault. Two rather curious features remain. In the first place she was full of heroin and secondly she was not a prostitute."

"She wasn't! But the clothes she was wearing, the contents of her bag. You're sure?"

"Yes, I'm sure, quite sure." He pulled on his coat, and then walked towards the door. Just before he reached it he turned and looked back at the policeman.

"You see, old man, I'm sure because I know. If you told me that she had a hundred things in her bag and was dressed like the Queen of Sheba with a price tag round her neck, I'd still be sure. She couldn't have been because according to my quite thorough examination, this little girl was a virgin."

Ellis walked across the saloon bar and laid the photograph on the counter.

"Ever seen her before?" he said, and for the third time that evening, waited for the shake of the head, the shudder and the quick handing back of the terrible picture.

Isaac Snow didn't shudder. His expression didn't change at all. He picked up the pasteboard in a hand like a flipper and held it carefully under the light. "Just let me think for a moment, Inspector," he said. "Just let me think."

He reached down to his side and then screwed an eyeglass into the folds of his face. He weighed about two hundred and eight pounds and apart from the collar was dressed like a clergyman. He had managed the "Castle Inn" for thirty years and people said he had seen better days. Ellis who had once had cause to examine the bank statements, doubted if that were possible. He looked like a very perverse Beardsley drawing.

"Yes, let me think. The poor child has been terribly disfigured, of course, and I would hate to commit myself in a court of law, but I rather think I do remember her. In fact I seem to feel that she may have been in this bar last night. Rather under the weather as I remember." He laid down the photograph and lifted his glass. He still smiled but his hand shook slightly and a few drops of liquid slopped down his dark waistcoat.

"Yes, I think she was in here last night. Couldn't have stayed long because I didn't really take her in. About nine o'clock I fancy, but we were pretty busy and my eyes are none too good. I may well be wrong. Let us see if one or more of our charming clientele can enlighten us."

He picked up the photograph and squeezed sideways through the flap of the bar. There was a peculiar feminine grace about his movements.

The "Castle" was a certain type of pub and its customers were types, too. They all carried the same air; a very quiet respectful air that hid a great deal. At the moment there were not many of them because it was only just after opening time and they all looked very well-behaved in Ellis's presence. Round the fire-place, three quiet youths in cloth caps and drain-pipe trousers studied the sporting papers and an old gentleman sat at the bar and smiled gently into his scotch and soda. He had a lot of white hair and pink cheeks and he looked a jolly old man. There was a long razor scar down the side of his face and his eyes didn't seem to focus quite correctly.

The rest of the customers were women and they were of every physical type; tall and short, dark and fair and ginger, lean and bloated. Most of them were middle aged. Ellis had been a long time in the Force and he knew half of them from years back. It made him wonder sometimes. It was supposed to be an unhealthy profession but most of these ladies looked remarkably fit and well.

Like an eighteenth-century buck, Snow moved among the elderly whores and with a smile and a word handed the pictures to each of them. Every time there came the wince, the shake of the head, the murmured "I never seen 'er, I wasn't in last night," and the hurried handing back of the photograph.

He was almost at the last table when his patience was rewarded. An enormous creature with a very tight costume and a port-wine mark down the side of her face stared at it, started and looked up at him.

"Yes, yes, I remember 'er, Mr. Snow. She was in here last night. Why I noticed that she was under the——" She broke off suddenly and glanced at Ellis.

"Come, come, Connie." Snow patted the bulging shoulder. "You mean that the young lady may have taken a little too much refreshment and was slightly intoxicated. You wish to protect the good name of the house. Very kind of you and I appreciate your loyalty, it does you credit. Still it is our duty as citizens to assist our good friends the police, and you must tell Mr. Ellis all you know. Inspector, may I introduce Mrs. Fowler. Connie to her friends, but trading under the name of Colline Claire. A romantic mixture of the Hibernian and the Gallic." Rather coyly Snow giggled.

"Good evening, Mrs. Fowler." Ellis pulled forward a chair and sat down in front of her. "You say you saw this girl in here last night. You're quite sure it was her. She wouldn't have looked quite the same then would she?"

"It was her all right, Inspector. I can recognize her." She still kept the photograph in her hand and stared at it. "Poor love. Somebody done 'er in and bashed 'er up as well." Her hard bloated face was oddly maternal. "You'll get the bastard who did it, won't you, Mr. Ellis?"

"Yes, we'll get him. Just as long as people like you come forward and help us, we'll get him. Now, what time was it that you saw her, Mrs. Fowler?"

"It was nine fifteen exactly. Tommy Stain had just finished on the tele. That's in the back room. I remember seeing him as I came through from powdering me nose. She was just coming in then. Sat down on the stool there. Funny you should ask me the time straight away, Mr. Ellis."

"Funny, why do you say that?" Ellis leaned forward towards her a little.

"I dunno exactly. It was her watch I think. She had a little gold watch on her wrist and she kept sort of showing it off. Waving her arm. I saw the time on it. It was dead right, just after nine fifteen. Almost as if she wanted everybody to see she had a watch."

"She did, did she?" Ellis took out his pocket book and made a note. "Was she alone?"

"Oh dear me no." Mrs. Fowler shook her head vigorously. "There was an old woman with her. That was what made me notice her at first. Proper old hag she was. Painted up like they'd dug 'er out of the grave and tried to make her decent. As I said, they sat up on the stools by the bar, which I personally think is rather vulgar for ladies. I remember remarking to me friend Eloise Goodman, that the girl looked as if she'd had a few. Kept leaning over towards the old woman and clutching her sort of."

"I see." Ellis's pencil travelled quickly down the page. It was fitting together. The girl wasn't drunk. The medical evidence was quite definite about that. There was not enough alcohol in her system to harm a child. There was something else. A large dose of heroin, which could well have made her lean over and clutch at her companion.

"Thank you, Mrs. Fowler. The couple came in about nine fifteen. The girl looked as if she was intoxicated and the old woman was very made up." He cleared his throat and looked suddenly embarrassed. "Would you—would you say that they belonged to your profession?"

"Oh yes. Sure of that, though where the old woman was concerned it would 'ave been a hell of a long time ago. Looked as if a good wind would 'ave blown 'er to bits. Funny I never seen her before. Thought I knew the lot by now." She took a large sip from her glass of port and lemon.

"Of course, I didn't pay much attention, and they didn't stay long. About twenty minutes it would have been. Then they went out with the feller."

"A fellow!" Ellis stiffened. "What fellow, Mrs. Fowler? Do you know him?"

"No, never seen 'im before. He was there when Eloise and I came in at about half past eight. Big chap, with very short dark hair. Sat all the time by the door there. Just one drink in front of him. Pint of bitter, I think it was. My friend Eloise suggested she gave him the eye, but I told 'er not to bother. Didn't look as if he had the price of another drink on 'im, let alone money for anything else. Besides he seemed to be waiting for someone."

"He did, did he? Did you get the impression he knew the two women?"

She frowned for a moment, and thought before answering. "I dunno, really. As I said, I wasn't paying a lot of attention. I seem to remember that he kept looking at 'em, but I can't be sure. It was rather odd how they left. Just after the half hour it would have been. The old girl finished her drink and then took the girl by the arm and led her towards the door. When they got there, she leaned over and said something to that chap. I didn't hear what it was but it worked all right. He finished his beer, got up like he was a soldier obeying the sergeant, held open the door for them, and they all went out together. I think that's all I can tell you, Mr. Ellis."

"And thank you, Mrs. Fowler, you've been most helpful. Just one more question and I've finished for the time being. This man. You say he was big with short dark hair. Was there anything else about him that would help us spot him. Clothes, for example; anything at all."

"No, not really. He had a dark suit on; grey I think it was, and pretty worn. He looked rather down at heel all round. Don't think there was anything else special about him. Just a minute though." She looked across at the table where the man had sat, and her forehead creased with concentration.

"Yes, Inspector, his hands. There was something the matter with his hands. He kept on sort of twisting 'em round his glass. Looked as if he couldn't help himself. Ruddy great mitts they was, and he had fingers on 'em that could fell a man."

"Damn! Damn! Damn!" Captain William Hailstone, R.N. retired, chief constable of the city, swore because he liked routine. He liked pickpockets to concentrate on pockets, cat burglars to shin forever up drainpipes and all types of criminals to remain types. Any deviation filled him with despair and fury. Now he glowered at the sheets of typescript in front of him and pulled savagely at a short, blackened pipe. It was empty and unlit because he was trying to stop smoking, but he liked the feel of it between his teeth.

"Yes, damn and blast it, Inspector. This whole business is wrong. Doesn't fit together, doesn't make sense, doesn't sound right. Just look at it." He pushed the papers away from him and pointed the pipe at Ellis like a revolver.

"Firstly, from the doctor, we know the girl was a virgin, yet she was got up like a low class prostitute. Why?

"Secondly, let's take the old woman. Who and what was she? Like the girl she appeared to be of a certain type and she spoke with a marked local accent. We've got the evidence of the barman for that. Yet nobody in the 'Castle Inn' recognized her. Why? The 'Castle' is probably the biggest den of thieves we've got, and in a town this size I would have thought that vice hung pretty closely together. Why wasn't she recognized?" At each "why" his pipe struck the edge of the desk with a sharp click.

"Finally, the man. From the nature of the attack it looks like the work of a psychopath, and as we know they're about as cunning and doggy as any type of criminal that exists. Yet what does this blighter do? Does he try any form of concealment? Not a bit of it. He sits in a crowded bar for everybody to look at him; he goes out with the woman quite openly. And then what—" Hailstone got up to the window, scowling out.

"You go on, Inspector, and give me the resumé again. This business is beginning to drive me barmy. Drunks who aren't drunks but full of dope: tarts who are virgins; sex maniacs who are chaste. Bah!"

"Yes, sir. I agree, it's all wrong." Ellis pulled the file over the desk and glanced at the second page.

"This man follows the two women out of the 'Castle,' and the three of them wait for a bus at the stop opposite. The time is exactly twenty-five to ten. The girl's watch was correct. The barman and Mrs. Fowler are both prepared to swear to that. At twenty to ten they get on a bus. It was a number 22 and the conductor took a good look at them because the girl seemed very drunk. She was swaying about at the stop and the man had to almost lift her on to the platform." Ellis broke off for a moment and watched the chief constable draw a red cross on the wall map.

"Right, they start out at the 'Castle,' here. During the journey they didn't speak to each other, I understand."

"No, sir. It seems odd, but the conductor was quite definite about it. The bus was almost empty and they sat on the end seats by the platform where he was standing. He paid particular attention to them because of the girl's condition. Seems he's got a daughter of his own and he was very shocked. He even saw the watch, too. It was right by the clock on the war memorial. The man said 'three fives' and gave him the exact fare. That was all they said. When they came to the Plaza cinema the old woman got off without a word."

"And the other two went on to the terminus." Once more Hailstone marked a point on the map. In the back of his mind he was watching the bus swaying home through the lighted streets with the conductor standing on the platform and thinking of his daughter, as he watched the silent trio on the platform. The girl lurching against the cushions; the old woman getting off at the cinema, and leaving her alone with the man and his restless hands.

"Yes, sir, to the Corn Market. The man had to help her off and they walked away with his arm round her shoulders. The conductor watched them go into the side turning."

"Yes, Patton Alley. A dead end that only leads to the steps down to the river where we found her. A very nice quiet area for him to pick. Almost deserted and all due for demolition as soon as the blasted council raises some money. What was the exact time the bus put them down? Ten to ten, thank you. And she was killed on the hour. The watch was broken by the same instrument he beat her with. A railway fish-plate that you found in the water near the body. There was blood on it and bits of glass from the watch. We can be almost sure of the time from that. Besides, we got that fellow on the tug. What was his name?"

"Naylor, sir."

"Yes, Skipper Naylor of the tug Famecock who was passing the backwater and heard a splash and running feet just as the cathedral clock began to strike the hour. Yes, we can allow him ten minutes from the time he got off the bus to the actual murder. Not long, but I suppose he could have done it." He stared at the map for a moment, pulled at his cold pipe and then went back to the desk.

"Well, he's made it all very nice and easy for you hasn't he, old boy? He even picks the one seat on the bus where the conductor will be bound to look at him. Almost as if he wanted it that way. Should be quite easy to trace him, but I wonder. I wonder a great deal. This lad may be a psychopath, but he's the rummiest one that's come my way. You've got no lead on the girl yet?"

"No, Sir. Only the ring. It seems it's foreign. German and fairly new. Don't know if it will help, but it might tell us something."

"Could be. Let's have a look at it." Hailstone leaned forward and took it from him. Under the light the metal snakes seemed to writhe and twist in his hand.

"Yes, German all right. Look at the lettering inside. I should say about two to three years old if she wore it constantly. Seventeen carat. Jewelry used to be a hobby of mine. Now what can it tell us. H.R. to G.R. in Gothic type. G.R. fits her name in her diary so it was probably bought for her when new. I'd like to know who Mr. H.R. is though." He spun the ring in his fingers and then flicked it across the table to Ellis.

"G.R. Gladys Reeves. If she brought it into the country it means that she had a passport and people with passports are not hard to trace. It might also mean something else. It might mean that she was a German."

"German, sir." Ellis risked a smile. "Gladys Reeves. The name's as British as they make 'em."

"Don't be a bloody fool, Inspector." Hailstone turned on him like a blight. "Names change, don't they. In particular German names. Ernst Hofmann becomes Ernest Hardy; Hans Steinberg, Henry Stonehill. They usually keep their initials though. Yes, I wonder if Gladys Reeves was once called something else?

"It may be a wild goose chase, but I want you to follow that line. Get on to the Immigration people. Find out if there are any little blond frauleins knocking about in this country who have initials G.R. and have also changed their addresses recently." He scowled as the telephone rang at his side and picked it up.

"Hailstone here. Yes, the inspector is with me. Hold on, I'll hand you over to him." He pushed the instrument across to Ellis and watched him take it.

"Hullo. What's that you say? Yes, of course, put her through at once." He laid his hand across the mouth-piece and turned to his chief.

"This might just be a break, sir. It's the woman Eloise Goodman, the friend of Mrs. Fowler. Says she's got something for us. Hullo, Mrs. Goodman, what can I do for you?"

"Good evening, Inspector." The voice was low and immensely genteel. In the background behind it he could hear a juke-box. It was playing "Stormy Weather."

"Inspector, I'm ringing you from the phone box in the 'Castle.' I've got something very important to tell you, but first I want your promise. I want your promise that you won't let on who tipped you off. I don't hold with murder, but I don't want the reputation of being an informer either."

"That's all right, Mrs. Goodman, you have my promise."

"Thank you, then listen carefully." The voice became lower, and more confidential. He could almost smell the rich gin fumes along the wire.

"If you want the fellow who took the girl out last night you'd better come round here. No, he's not in the bar, but he's outside. I can see him through the window, standing watching the door. You'd better hurry, he's been there ten minutes already."

"Thank you very much, Mrs. Goodman." Ellis pressed down the phone rest and spoke to the desk sergeant. His voice was very harsh and urgent as he gave his orders. Then he looked at Hailstone.

"You heard, sir?"

"Yes, I heard." He got up from his chair and knocked his pipe over the waste paper basket. It was quite clean already but the action helped him to think.

"Yes, I heard. The joker's gone back to the scene of his crime has he? Very obliging of him. I know they're supposed to do that in fiction, but in this case it's just a little too quick. Too quick, and much too simple." He looked at the map again and he cursed under his breath.

"You know, old boy, I'm beginning to get a feeling about this case. A most unpleasant feeling. Get through to the Immigration people at once will you, and when they bring our friend in, I want to see him. Yes, I'm beginning to feel that our murder may not have been the end of an affair, but just the beginning. A very nasty beginning to something worse."

He watched Ellis take up the phone again and then looked out of the window at the mist drifting over the city. A dark city with its tall bridges and grey river, and here and there the lights of a ship on the river. The lights of ships and the lights of the pubs with their brass fittings and juke boxes and elderly whores inside, and outside a man watching.

"Yes," he said. "Curiouser and curiouser isn't it, Alice?"

Outside there came a burst of bells, as a car turned out of the yard to bring him Big Hands.

CHAPTER TWO

"*Half a pound of twopenny rice, half a pound of treacle. That's the way the money goes*—Bang!" said General Kirk of British Foreign Intelligence, as he squinted along the barrels of his twelve bore shot-gun and pulled the trigger. Had the gun been loaded it would have blown the head from a signed photograph of Sir Winston Churchill.

"Got you." He lowered the gun and grinned at Michael Howard, his first assistant.

"Well, Mike. It's all yours now. For three weeks you will be in complete charge of this miserable department, while I spend my time attempting to slaughter perfectly inoffensive birds. Yes, freedom for three weeks. Hey ding ding a ding."

He thrust the gun into a vulgar tartan case and pulled up the zip fastener. He wore thick green tweeds and a deer-stalker hat, that over-emphasized his heavy cynical features. He looked like one of Buchan's aristocratic villains, plotting a very low blow against the Crown.

"First time for years isn't it, sir?" Michael Howard smiled back at him. He was a tall, untidy man, with a mild academic expression. It was a very studied expression, but it worked well as long as you didn't look too hard into his eyes.

"Yes. To be exact, Mike, the first time for ten years. Never had the opportunity before. Always some damned thing came cropping up to stop me. Now everything's quiet and I'm grabbing the chance. You'll be able to manage all right won't you?"

"Of course, sir. Apart from that chap in Albania, there doesn't seem much to worry about. I'll keep you informed if anything out of the way crops up. You've left your phone number, just in case?"

"Yes, Nantwood 375. Care of Fetherstone Clumber-Holt Esquire. A miserable old bastard I went to school with, but he owns one of the best grouse moors in the country, and it's the twelfth of August tomorrow." He stuck an enormous cigar into his mouth, lit it, and picked up the gun-case.

"Well, bye bye, Mike. Keep my seat warm."

"Goodbye, sir, and good hunting. Send me a couple of brace if you can." Michael moved to open the door for him and then paused as the phone rang.

"Excuse me a moment," he said, and picked it up. "Hullo, this is Room 17. Just a minute, I'll see." He looked up, and grinned at Kirk's head shake. "No, I'm very sorry, but the general has left. No, I don't expect he will be back for at least three weeks. Perhaps I can help you. I see." His voice changed suddenly and all the mildness went out of his eyes.

"The devil you say. Dead is she, and you're almost certain as to the identity. Yes, of course we're interested, very interested indeed. Just hold the line while I get a pencil." He laid the phone down on the table and looked up at Kirk.

"It's the Immigration Office, sir. They were asked to check the identity of a girl by the Minechester police. She was murdered there the night before last. Found in the river almost cut to pieces. On the surface, it doesn't look like our show, but it just may be. They're not certain yet, but it seems possible that this girl was Gerda Raine."

"Damn! Gerda Raine, eh. This may make me miss my train." The general leaned his gun against the wall and picked up the phone.

"Hullo, this is Kirk here. Please tell me all you know about this business. What's that you say? No, I've not gone away for three weeks. I'm speaking to you now and I don't give a damn what my assistant has told you. Yes, I've got a ruddy pencil. Just get on with it, man."

For perhaps five minutes he listened to the voice on the line, then he growled his thanks and replaced the phone.

"Well, Mike, it seems that this just may be something for us. They aren't sure yet, but it sounds as if it was Gerda Raine, though she had been calling herself Gladys Reeves. She was wearing a curious ring which I seem to remember. If it was Gerda, then I want to know exactly how and why she died. I want to know that very much, Mike." For a moment his left hand, that was terribly scarred and lacked three fingers, drummed quietly on the electric radiator that glowed in the corner of the room.

"You never saw her, did you?"

"No, sir. I was in the States at the time. I remember you describing her though. You said she had a pretty, hard little face, and it might have belonged to somebody else."

"Did I? Quite the poet. She won't be pretty now, though. Soft or hard, they never look pretty when they're dead." He glanced up at the big wall clock in front of him.

"Well, I suppose you'd better look into it. I don't really believe that our friends have a full scale murder organization operating in this country, but if they have, I can imagine that little Miss Raine would be quite high on the list as a potential victim. You'd better get her identified in any case. Tell you what, that young woman of yours could help. When you were in the States I let her do some work here. She was very cut up about that wretched business of her brother, and I think it did her good. An efficient creature too. She'd know Gerda again.

"Now, I've an hour before my train. I was hoping for a meal on the way, but that'll have to be skipped now. As you weren't here, I'd better go through the files with you. Get them for me, will you, Mike. Gerda Raine's and Hugh Richmond's as well."

He sat down at the desk as Michael fetched the files and pulled hard at his cigar. The grey smoke rose to the ceiling, hung there for a moment, and then drifted away like the trail of the lost years.

"Put them here," he said as Michael came back, "and sit down. We'll go through this story as quickly as we can, then it'll be up to you to find the end of it." He pulled over the first folder and opened it.

"Yes, Hugh Richmond. Captain Hugh Richmond. Number 65793 B. Royal Engineers. Aged thirty-eight and still a captain. Due for redundancy at any moment. Nothing at all interesting about this dull, weak and very foolish man, except that because he was foolish he made a mistake. A bad mistake. Take a look at him, son."

He pushed a photograph across to Michael, and watched him look at the long, heavy face, with its pale eyes, pencil moustache and an expression that could be seen in every barracks, mess or requisitioned house, where British regular officers are stationed.

"Richmond was in charge of a filing office attached to our Berlin H.Q. He spent his time, quite efficiently it seems, sorting out leave permits, travel warrants, barrack accounts; all that type of thing. It looks as if he would have carried on like that till they gave him the boot and then he had a bit of bad luck. Somebody made a mistake. A crashing mistake. An envelope was misdirected and it arrived at Richmond's office. It contained a document intended for the general. A really hot document for it gave a full list of our proposed rocket sites in Western Europe.

"Well, that was the beginning. If Richmond had been slightly more intelligent, it wouldn't have mattered. He would have taken it personally to headquarters at once and forgotten he had ever seen it. He didn't. It was almost time to shut up his office and he had an appointment with his girl that he wanted to keep. He did the most foolish thing in his life. He locked that top secret, most vital document in his desk and went off to meet her."

"And she was Gerda Raine?"

"Yes, Mike. She was Gerda Raine." Kirk took out another picture and looked at a pretty, blonde face with wide blue eyes and a bitter mouth. "Gerda Raine, a German waitress employed at a cafe in the Fehrberliner Platz, not far from Richmond's office and also something else."

"Yes, sir. I'm beginning to remember the story. She was a VOPO agent wasn't she?"

"Yes, she was a free lance agent attached to the East German People's Police, but she was also rather more important. She was on the direct payroll of our old friend Comrade Peter Kun, who in those days was in charge of Soviet Army Intelligence in Germany."

"I see." Michael whistled slightly as he thought of Peter Kun. The best secret service organizer the Russians had got and at the moment not ten minutes walk away from their office. Employed ostensibly in some junior capacity, but doubtless with his fingers on some very important and sinister strings.

"As many weak men will, Richmond puffed up his ego by boasting to women. He told Gerda about the papers and said they had been sent to him personally. She was very, very interested. Clever about it as well. It appears that he hadn't slept with her yet, but was trying to work up to it. She played on his vanity. Told him he was merely lying to impress her and she didn't believe a word of it. She got him to drink a good deal as well, and at last brought on a fit of temporary insanity.

"Richmond lost his temper, dragged her out of the cafe to his car and drove her to the office. Five minutes later he was showing her that vital document. He was altogether very helpful. Even provided her with a weapon. He was in some wretched hockey team and kept his bat, or whatever you call them, in the office. It seems to have made quite a useful club. Very soon afterwards, little Miss Raine was in a taxi on her way to the Russian sector of the city."

"But she didn't cross the border did she, sir?" Michael leaned over and took the photograph. "She had something to sell first, hadn't she?"

"Oh, yes, she had something to sell. To the highest bidder. It appears that for some time she had been finding life with Peter Kun and the VOPO a little tedious. She took the papers to a phone booth near the border by the Brandenburg Tor and there she made two calls. One was to our pal Kun at the Russian H.Q. and the other to us. We don't know what she said to the Russians, but her terms to us were quite moderate. Amnesty for what she had done, five hundred pounds and last but not least, a British passport within twenty-four hours. They had one hour to agree to them."

"Yes, as you say, pretty moderate." Michael raised his eyebrows slightly. "Our people granted them of course."

"They granted them at once. What else could they do? If the Russians had got hold of those papers it would have been a hell of a mess. Richmond had come round by then and rung through to them. They knew Gerda was speaking the truth. General Whitman was almost dragged out of a cocktail party to sign the necessary promise she asked for, and they sent a car to pick her up. She was flown out of Berlin the same night and some clot gave me the job of looking after her. She didn't want any protection, though. Seemed quite capable of looking after herself. Three years ago it must have been, yes, almost three years to the very day."

He leaned back in his chair and thought of the girl coming into the room. On the surface an ordinary girl, who you would hardly notice in a crowd, a rather appealing childlike girl but behind the child something that was very hard and bitter and efficient. Something that was so strong that he could almost smell it. Fear. He could still remember her exact words to him.

"No, Herr General, I do not require a body-guard. All I want from you is the passport that I have been promised, and the right to disappear. You see, I don't think you could protect me, if you set a guard over me till my dying day."

Her dying day. That was the day before yesterday. He pulled back his chair and stood up.

"Well, son," he said, "it's all yours. We know nothing at the moment and this may well be a purely domestic crime and the business of the police. If so, leave it alone; but if not, I want to know about it. All about it. Remember that this girl once betrayed Dr. Kun, and I don't think he would like that. He wouldn't like it at all, and if he is running a murder organization in this country it's up to us to break it, and quickly. Take Penny with you and have a talk with Minechester police. If you think it has anything to do with us you might look me up. Old Clumber-Holt's place is only a few miles from there as it happens and he keeps some quite drinkable port." He tightened his coat, picked up the gun, and adjusted his terrible hat.

"Anything else you want to know before I hook it, Mike?"

"Just one thing, sir." Michael rummaged among the papers. "What happened to Richmond? It doesn't seem to be in the file."

"No, it wouldn't be. As far as we were concerned the thing finished with the recovery of the papers. Let me see though, I did hear something. Yes, that's right. They were going to court-martial him but he beat them to it. The bloody fool didn't even make a job of it. Blew half his jaw off, I think, and took five hours to bleed to death. Bye bye, Mike. I must go now."

"Goodbye, sir. Have a nice time." Michael watched his boss move through the door towards Fetherstone Clumber-Holt's drinkable port and the glorious twelfth of August. Then he took up the phone and asked to be connected with the Minechester police. When at last he put it down, his hard eyes were very thoughtful. For about half an hour he flicked over the papers that Kirk had left on his desk, then he picked up his coat and went out of the building.

Penny Wise ran a second-hand motor business at the end of a Bayswater mews. It was not a very large or imposing concern but it seemed to pay cash and the rent. She was a fine big girl, with a lot of fair hair that looked dyed, but wasn't, and she was standing quite still at the back of the yard gazing with near reverence at one of the most repulsive vehicles that Michael had ever seen. It took her all her time to look away from it as he walked towards her.

"Hullo, darling," she said. "Just look and gape and envy me for a moment. Isn't she wonderful?"

"Well, I suppose if you like that sort of thing." Michael stood back and regarded the paragon. It looked about a hundred years old and ten feet high. There was an unpleasant sneering expression from its enormous concave hood and it was coated with faded blue paint and a thick film of rust.

"Just what is it supposed to be?"

"Don't be so damned blasé, Mike. For one thing she's my pay ticket for the next twelve months. A real collector's piece and quite unique. The only type that was ever built. Alfredo Bugatti's sole venture into the non-sports field. Specially hand built for some oriental prince or other and now rescued by me from a barn in Dorset. Paint her, tune her up, clean the mice nests out of the upholstery and the boys will come running."

"I see. Very beautiful. Now that I've admired it, what about a drink?" He put an arm round her shoulders and led her up to the little flat above the garage.

"Cheers, darling." Penny sipped her gin and then leaned forward and kissed him on the lips. "Over a week since you've been round. Busy?"

"So, so. The old man's gone on holiday and I'm holding the fort for him." He smiled at her and cupped his hand over her right breast.

"Tell me," he said. "When are you going to marry me?"

"Soon, darling, very soon." She ran her fingers over his hand, pressing it against her. "Just as soon as my poor, wretched husband shuffles off these mortal coils. Won't be very long. The poor lamb is doing all he can to help I gather. Fell down the stairs of his club, dead drunk, yesterday. Can't keep that up for long." She leaned back for a moment and grinned at him.

"Tell me, Mike. There's a nasty expression in your eyes. A business expression. Have you come here for the sake of my bonny brown hair or for something else?"

"Sorry, Penny, something else. I want a little help in identification from you. Recognize this?" He held the photograph out to her.

"Let's have a look." She took the picture and held it in front of her, frowning slightly. Her eyes suddenly grew very cold and her full mouth drooped slightly.

"Yes, of course I recognize her, Mike. Gerda Raine, isn't it. What's the little bitch done now?"

"She's done nothing, nothing at all this time. Just died. It seems that somebody helped her quite a lot. It may not be our affair but we have to be sure. I gather you didn't approve. The old man seemed to rather like her."

"Yes, the old man, as you call him might have done. Kirk has just one pet aversion in his life; failures. To him, people like Richmond are perfectly fair game and as long as they are neat and clever about it he rather approves of creatures like Gerda Raine, even when they happen to be on the other side." She wrinkled her nose at the photograph and dropped it on the table in front of them.

"So, she's dead is she? Good. To me she seemed a very nasty piece of work. I remember talking to her in your office. As you know, Kirk gave me a sort of general runabout job when you were in America. I came in to give her the passport they had promised and then I told her that Richmond had killed himself. She drew her fingers over the passport, as if it were the most beautiful thing she had ever handled, and then she looked up at me and smiled.

"'How foolish of him,' she said, 'but then, he was a fool, wasn't he? You know, Mrs. Wise'—she pronounced it with a V, and she had one of those phoney American accents they sport in Germany since the war—'you know, Mrs. Vise, this reminds me of one of Napoleon's maxims. Surely you remember what he said: To make an omelette it is necessary to break an egg. To me, Captain Richmond was just an egg, but this; my dear Mrs. Vise'—she smiled at the passport as she tucked it into her bag. 'This is my omelette.'

"Tell me, Mike, who did it?"

"We don't know who, yet, just how. A very nasty how. It seems somebody filled her up with dope, dressed her as a street walker, cut her to ribbons and threw her in the river." He broke off and scowled at Penny.

"For God's sake, stop laughing, girl. It's not in the least funny. It's horrible."

"But it is funny, Mike. It's damned funny. Just the kind of death I would have thought suitable for Fräulein Gerda. Who is this paragon of murderers, I would like to meet him."

"You may do. As I said, this may be our show and in any case, I want you to identify the body. We don't know why she died yet, but I can think of one person with a good reason for hating her and his name is Peter Kun."

"Yes, Peter Kun. Kirk told me about him. He's good, isn't he." For a moment her face grew serious, like a child mentioning the bogey-man. "Yes, he had a reason all right. They don't like their own traitors do they? Tell me, where did she die?"

"Minechester. I want to go up there tonight, so go and tell your manager that you are going to desert him for a bit, and then start getting ready."

"Minechester, eh. Cor, just the sort of dump she would pick to die in. I've got an idea though. We'll take the Bugatti. Just the sort of run she needs as a test. No—" she broke off sadly as she watched Michael shake his head.

"No, not the Bugatti. I want to live and I have no desire to arrive like part of the circus coming to town. We'll take the night train. I think the department will run to a couple of first class sleepers."

"Thank you, sir. That will be most romantic. Just you and me on the Scotch express. I'll go and tell Tony, then. Back in a moment."

"Don't be long." Michael watched her go out of the door, then he picked up the photograph and stared at it as he finished his gin. Even with her anonymous face and her thin bitter mouth, Gerda Raine had once been rather beautiful.

"Poor little blonde girl," he said. "Somebody must have really hated you mustn't they?" He pushed it away from him and leaned back on the sofa twirling the empty glass in his hand. All the time his eyes kept flicking over to the picture.

"Yes, they must have hated you," he said, "but they shouldn't have done that to you. You may have been a prize bitch but they shouldn't have killed you that way."

He got up and glanced at his watch. It was getting on for ten. Nearly forty eight hours had passed since Big Hands had walked down the steps to the river.

CHAPTER THREE

Captain Hailstone carefully closed the door of the mortuary behind him and looked at Penny.

"Well, little lady, do you think it's her?"

Penny didn't answer him for a moment. She leaned against the wall and shut her eyes. She was breathing deeply, and even under her make-up she looked pale and drawn.

"Yes, I think so," she said. "I can't be quite certain because she's been so terribly mutilated, but I think that was Gerda Raine. I can remember the ring quite distinctly. She was wearing it on the two occasions I saw her."

"Thank you, my dear. That's fair enough for the time being and you've been very brave about it. It wasn't a nice sight." He patted her shoulder and grinned. "Now, let's get on back to my den and have a drink. I expect you could both use one. Quite certain I can."

Hailstone's den was a dark gloomy room packed with sporting trophies. On every wall, shelf and table, tarnished cups and shields testified to his former athletic prowess. Over the mantelpiece there was a rugger ball in a glass case. A notice below it read "H.M.S. Athene R.F.C. Home Fleet championship 1934-5," and there was a picture of Hailstone himself, in a comical tasselled cap beside it. He waved them into deep leather chairs and pulled an amber bottle and glasses out of a cupboard.

"Well, God bless. Now, I'm extremely grateful to you both for coming up and helping to identify the body, but I'm afraid it has been a bit of a fruitless journey. You see, I think we've broken it, and to me it looks like a very simple nut killing. No chance of a 'Commie' plot at all. Yes, it's all tied up, bar the shouting. Here, have a look at it for yourself, Howard." He pushed a folder of typescript across the desk to Michael.

"Thank you, sir." Michael read through them quickly and then passed the notes back to him.

"So you think that's it, do you, sir. You think this chap Carlton must be your man?"

"I do more than think, old boy. I'm quite certain about it in my own mind. Cut and dried case from the beginning. Let's look at the facts.

"The murdered girl was a foreigner who came to this town a little over a month ago. She took a job as a domestic servant with a Mrs. Brett, who lives in Popes Grove. Very nice street, Popes Grove. Quite the best part of the town. Live near there myself. As far as she can tell us, Mrs. Brett said the girl seemed to have no friends and rarely went out. She was quite willing and good at her work, but seemed bored. After two weeks she leaves without giving any reason. Just collects her pay, packs her bag and goes.

"Well, we don't know yet where she went but I'm sure it wouldn't be to such a nice area of the town. Yes, all cut and dried." He finished his drink and pulled at his cold pipe.

"You see, I've seen it, Howard. Seen it so many times. Girls like that do get bored and discontented. They begin to think of easy money and if they have no friends and relations to turn to, they drift into bad company and finally they go on the game. It's all a very simple pattern. This girl may have been a virgin but there's always a first time, and from the description of the woman who took her to the "Castle Inn," I should say that she found a friend who encouraged her in her way of life with the judicious use of a little heroin. Fair enough, Howard?"

"Perhaps, sir. It might have been like that but I wonder." As Michael had listened to him he knew that it couldn't have been like that. He knew that it was wrong, completely wrong. Whatever the facts, it couldn't have been that way because of the character of Gerda Raine herself. She wasn't a simple girl who would be exploited by any provincial vice ring. She was a very hard, clever girl indeed, and she knew exactly how to take care of herself.

"And the man, sir. What about him. What's he like?"

"You'll see for yourself in a moment. We've got him downstairs. Haven't got much out of him, but we don't need to. He's as guilty as hell and we have all the witnesses we need to prove it. The people in the bar and the bus conductor. He was seen walking towards the steps at ten to ten and she was killed at ten exactly. The watch was stopped then and the skipper of the barge is prepared to swear that he heard the splash and running feet, just as the cathedral clock struck the hour. Good enough for you?"

"Yes, sir, it seems like it. It seems that you may have got the killer, but before I'm quite certain I think we should know a little more about the victim." He drained his glass and stood up. "All right if we take a look at Carlton?"

"Of course. The officer outside will show you the way. I doubt if you'll find friend Carlton very talkative, but it may help you to see what I mean. He's just the type we always find in this sort of affair. Psychopath if ever there was. Come back and let me know what you think in any case."

He held open the door for them, beamed once more at Penny, and watched them follow the uniformed constable towards the cells.

The big man sat quite still on his iron cot and he might have been there forever. On the day that the old building was completed he might have been forgotten and left behind by the workmen, and sat quite still waiting for somebody to come and collect him and take him home. But nobody had come, so he had sat there alone till he had become part of the structure itself, with its cells and its walls and the bars in the walls that gave him a little glimpse at the sky.

He looked out at the city through the bars and the plastic panes of the window and he was like the city too; very old and big and tired; terribly tired. Only his hands were young as they twisted and untwisted over the serge of his shabby suit. The rest of him was old and there was no bed, no sleep that could ever wipe out the weary lines from his old, tired face. His name was James Carlton and he was aged nineteen.

Michael looked at him through the peep-hole and then spoke to the warder. As the door opened, he motioned to Penny to follow him and then walked through into the cell.

Carlton didn't look up. He just sat where he was, hunched on his cot and for all the interest he showed, they might not have been there. Only his hands seemed to notice them. They stopped moving and lay quite still on his knees. They seemed to be waiting for something.

Michael leaned against the wall opposite him but he didn't look at him, he looked at Penny. She sat down on the cot beside Carlton and crossed her legs. She left a lot of them showing.

"Hullo, James," she said and smiled at him. "Would you like to talk to us for a moment?"

Very slowly the big man raised his head and looked towards her. He was like a bear. Not shaggy, not rough, for his hair was cut very short, almost shaven, but there was something lumbering and ungainly and bear-like about him. For perhaps five seconds he looked at her face and then his eyes dropped lower and his head sunk back to its former position.

"Quite right, James, you don't want to talk to any more girls do you?" Michael reached in his pocket and pulled out his cigarette case.

"You're in quite enough trouble from girls already. Talk to me, though. I'm not a policeman, you know, and oddly enough, I'm rather on your side at the moment." He reached out the case and held it towards Carlton with one cigarette pointing forward.

"Go on, take it," he said. "It may make you feel a little better."

"Ta." As if it were taking something dangerous, the big, restless hand reached out and lifted the cigarette from the pack. When it was lit, he dragged greedily at it but he didn't inhale.

"Yes, that's better isn't it, James. Gives you a bit of confidence." Michael sat down beside him and smiled. Somehow his smile was very personal to Carlton and seemed to exclude Penny. "Now, let's see what we know about you." He reached in his pocket once more and this time brought out Hailstone's notes.

"Yes, here we are. Your name is James Carlton, and you live with your mother, in Number 15 Shelley Avenue. That's right, isn't it? Let's go on. You were nineteen your last birthday, yet you have never once held a steady job. I wonder why that is, James. Still, it's not my business. A lot of people don't work and you've never been in any real trouble, have you? Not until last Wednesday night. The night of Wednesday, August the ninth, when the police say you went out and killed a girl. I wonder if that's true, James. Want to tell me about it?" He leaned forward, till his face was almost touching Carlton's, but there was no answering expression from those old, tired eyes.

"Come on, James, you'd better talk about it. You see, the police have got all the facts they need and all the witnesses. Lots of witnesses. The people in the bar, where you met the girl and the old woman, the bus conductor who took you to the terminus, even the skipper of a tug boat who was passing at that time and heard the splash. They've got you all wrapped up it seems. Besides she marked you, didn't she. Just before you killed her, she gave you something. This—"

His hand shot out and took Carlton's, twisting the palm uppermost. At the end of the wrist there were three long, ragged scratches.

"Yes, she put her mark on you, James, so that we could recognize you. That is the last piece of evidence we needed. I'm almost sure you killed her, James, but there's one thing I'm not sure about. Tell me, who ordered you to kill her?"

And that went home. For the first time Carlton's eyes showed a flicker of interest and his head moved towards Michael.

"Don't go on, mister," he said. "Please don't go on. I don't mind what you do to me, but please leave me alone. I don't care what happens any more. I never harmed that girl at all and nobody made me do anything to her, but don't go on at me. Hang me if you like, but please leave me alone."

"Don't worry, James, they won't hang you. They won't be allowed to hang you; they'll just be very nice to you. They'll feed you and clothe you and put you away where you'll be quite safe. I wonder if you can remember the old nursery rhyme. How does it go? Yes, 'We'll catch a fox and put him in a box and never let him go.'"

He smiled at the boy and there was nothing nice about his smile. "Yes," he said very gently. "And shut him in a box and never let him go."

And that time it worked. It went home right in the center of the target and Carlton changed. A dark flush came into his face and he stood up. His big hands reached out and gripped Michael's coat.

"You mean they'll put me away?" His voice was quite controlled on the surface, but there was a lot of fear behind it. "They wouldn't do that, would they, mister? They can't do that. They haven't the right to do that."

"They can, they will, and believe me they have the right." Once more Michael gave him his friendly, unfriendly smile. "That is of course unless you'd like to tell me about it." He watched Carlton's hands fall to his sides and he sat down.

"Good. Now, let's start at the beginning, shall we? It seems that you had never been in the 'Castle' before that night. Why did you go there then?"

"It was bright, mister. I was just walking past and it looked so bright. Besides I could hear music."

"I see. You like music and the pub looked bright, so you went in and bought yourself a glass of bitter beer. Do you like beer, James?"

"Yes, I like it very much. But I don't tell anybody. You see mother told me that that was the way my father started before he, he—died. That night Mrs. Green had given me five shillings for cutting her wood. I gave three to Mother. But—two I kept for myself." His voice lowered slightly and he might have been repeating the worst secret in the world.

"Right. You had two shillings in your pocket so you went into the bar and bought yourself a pint of bitter. That would come to one and ninepence wouldn't it. Threepence left. Quite sure that was all the money you had on you?"

Carlton nodded his head vigorously and checked as his eyes came into the arc of Penny's legs.

"Good, let's get on then. Why did you speak to the old woman with the girl?"

"I didn't, I never spoke to her. She came over to me. She told me she wanted me to go outside with them. She said the girl was ill and she couldn't get her home by herself. She said I had to help. There was to have been somebody at the top of the steps to the river waiting to meet her. I took her there, mister, and that's all I did. I had to do what that old lady told me. I dunno why, but there was something about her that made me do it." He bent his head and stared at the floor.

"I see." Michael looked at his bowed head and all at once he knew that however strange it might seem, Carlton was telling the truth. It had been just like that. The old woman had told him to do something and he had done what she told him. Out of all the people of the city she had picked the one person who would obey her. The slow-witted boy with the guilty secret. Two shillings which he had hidden from his widowed mother.

"Very well. She gave you the exact money and you took the bus. She got off at the Plaza and left you alone with the girl. You took her to the top of the steps where she was to be met and you waited. But there wasn't anybody to meet her, was there, James? And now you're going to tell me exactly what happened." His hand shot out suddenly, grasping Carlton's hair and pulling his head backward till he was looking at him.

"Now, you great dumb bastard, tell me about it. Tell me what happened on the river steps."

"Nothing, nothing at all. She scratched me. She leaned against the wall and I felt she was going to fall. I held her up and then she scratched me. Here." His fingers ran along the lines of his wrist and there were tears in his eyes. "Then I saw the two men with the dog and I was frightened so I left her."

"Yes, you told the police about that, didn't you. You said that you saw two elderly men coming up the steps in front of you. You said you were frightened of their seeing you with the girl so you ran away."

"I said something like that, but you've got it wrong, all wrong." His head jerked away from Michael's hand and for a moment he felt the strength of Carlton.

"I didn't run. I just wanted to get away from the girl because she'd scratched me. I left her and walked in front of the men. I felt safe with them. Little white dog they had with them. No bigger than a rabbit it was. I walked in front of them all the way to the main road and then I went home."

"Yes, then you went home. That's the one thing we know you did, because we have the evidence of your mother. She says you arrived home at twenty past ten and went straight to bed. Now, let's try and think about those two men you say you saw. Do they really exist or are they only in your mind? The police haven't been able to trace them, you see, and it shouldn't be difficult to find two elderly men with a little white dog. Tell me, James. Do they exist?" Once more his hand pulled the head backwards.

"I dunno. I just don't know. I thought so at the time, but now I'm not sure. I forget things you see. I always forget things." His head was heavy and without resistance now. Only Michael's hand held it up.

"Yes, you forget things. Do you forget what you did the next day? You went back and stood outside the public house, didn't you? Just why did you do a foolish thing like that, James?"

"To say I was sorry, of course. I'd left the girl, hadn't I? I hadn't waited for anybody to meet her."

"Yes, you'd left the girl, so you went back to the 'Castle' to see if you could find her and say you were sorry."

"No, not her. You don't understand. I didn't like the girl and I didn't want to see her again. It was the other one I wanted to see. The old lady. I had to tell the old lady I'd let her down."

"Very well, that's all for the moment." Michael released his head and stood up. He beckoned to Penny and looked once more at Carlton, but he didn't say another word to him. Then he called to the warder and they went out.

When they had gone Carlton sat quite still, looking at the peep-hole in the door. As soon as he was sure he was not being watched he went down on his knees and turned towards the bed. He laid his face against it and slowly his hands came up and his fingers began to knead and tear at the rough blanket. They were exactly on the place where Penny had been sitting.

"Won't keep you a moment, old man." Hailstone grinned at Michael and then turned to the woman sitting beside his desk. She was dressed in black and was terribly small. Her feet barely reached the floor and she looked like a dwarf beside Hailstone.

"Well, ma'm, there's nothing for you to worry about at the moment. I'll see that your son gets fixed up with legal aid. Just one point more and I'm finished. I understand that you've been his sole support for the last seventeen years."

"Yes, sir. I've looked after James all the time since my husband—died." There was a slight pause between the words.

"Thank you, then, that's all I need for the moment." Hailstone got up and held open the door for her.

"Goodbye, Mrs. Carlton, and please, don't worry. Your son isn't a criminal, but merely sick. He won't be punished, just helped and looked after. Please try and remember that." He watched her walk away; a very small and pathetic figure in the long corridor, then he turned to Michael.

"Well, Howard, that's the lot. No doubt left. That woman was the mother and even she seems to believe he did it. Seems there's a long history of mental disease in the family. The father was very odd. Two years after the boy was born he went off the rails completely; drink, drugs, women, the lot in fact. Because of that, James has a deep-seated fear and horror of women of a certain type. There's your motive. Quite satisfied at last?"

Michael shook his head and smiled at him. "'Fraid not, sir. I'm not satisfied at all. Carlton may be a psychopath, I rather think he is; his story doesn't ring true and he was almost certainly with the girl right up to the time of the murder; the mother has provided a satisfactory motive. It all fits, but I'm still not satisfied. I want to know a lot more. Thank you." He took a cigarette from the box that Hailstone pushed across to him, lit it and went on.

"You see, although Carlton may have done the actual murder, I feel he was just a pawn in somebody else's hands and I want to know about that somebody. For instance, who was the old woman who took the girl to the bar, and who seems to have such a strong personality. Your white-slave theory falls flat you know. They might have doped the girl and they might have looked for an outside pick-up to start her on her new way of life, but it wouldn't have been James Carlton with two shillings in his pocket. Oh no, not on your life."

"Yes, I see your point, old boy, but so what! Although I'd very much like to bring in that authoritative old lady, I fancy I've got the chap I want, the real killer. I think she just made a mistake and picked the wrong man. No, there's no deep dark plot here, but just a sordid little tragedy. As to that story about the two men and the dog, that's just rubbish, Carlton's subconscious working overtime to produce an alibi." He moved to his cupboard and once again produced the bottle.

"Now, we'll have a final drink together and then I expect you and your very charming assistant will want to go back to town." He smirked at Penny as he said it.

"Thank you, sir, but I think we'll stay till tomorrow, you know. As I said, I want to know a good deal more before I write this off as not our business. Cheers." He drank his whisky in one go and put the glass on the desk.

"It doesn't fit together you see, sir. None of it does. We knew Gerda Raine and she wasn't like the person you suggest. She wasn't a bit like it. She wasn't the type to be a domestic servant, and she certainly was not the type to become a small-time tart. No, there's something else behind this murder; a very well planned and nasty something else.

"I think that Gerda came up here because she was frightened and I think she took that menial job as a hiding place. I think she left it for the same reason. If you discover where she went after Mrs. Brett, I think you will find it was a very low class lodging house. You see, the lower you go in accommodation, the more anonymous you become. That girl, sir, was terrified of something and she was trying to run away from it. Unfortunately she didn't run far enough and it caught up with her."

He stopped as the door opened and a policewoman came into the room. She laid a note on Hailstone's desk and she went out without speaking.

"Now, what the devil is this about? I told them I wasn't to be disturbed unless it was urgent." He put on a pair of thick glasses and picked up the paper. As he read, a look of complete bewilderment came into his face.

"Good God!" His voice was somehow quite different and he took a stiff pull at his glass. "Well, well, that's that. My apologies, Howard. It seems that you're right and we're wrong. Carlton is in the clear. Take a look at it for yourself."

Michael grinned at the paper, but didn't look at it at once. "Let me try to guess, sir," he said. "I hate to be wise after the event but I think I know what this says. Carlton is in the clear because those two men with their dog turned up. That's it, isn't it?" He picked up the paper and started to read.

"Yes, all very nice and tidy, and he seems to have told the exact truth. They came up the steps and saw him. He left the girl by the wall and walked in front of them all the way to the main road. Good reliable witnesses too. I see that one of them is a local magistrate. Well, Carlton is out, but I wonder who is in. What a lot of trouble they've taken though. Do you remember what Napoleon said, sir?"

"Napoleon? What on earth has that fellow got to do with this?"

"Nothing really, sir. It was just something he said. Something that Gerda Raine once quoted. 'To make an omelette, it is necessary to break an egg.'" He ground out his cigarette and stood up.

"Yes," he said, "and what a lot of trouble they've taken. What a lot of trouble to break this one little egg."

CHAPTER FOUR

Fetherstone Clumber-Holt Esquire, M.C., J.P., and chairman of a dozen companies, sat at the end of a vast mahogany table with a copy of "The Field" propped up in front of him. He was eating bacon, eggs, sausage, kidneys and a mutton chop. He growled to himself as he read and at his feet a bear-like Labrador wheezed in sympathy. From every corner of the big dark room, foxes, otters and red-deer gazed sadly at him; while through the window a bleak expanse of moorland stretched west through stunted pine trees and thin summer rain. He turned a page of the magazine, snorted loudly and swung round as the door behind him opened.

"Ah, there you are, old chap. Come on in and help yourself to some grub. Should be still hot. All on the sideboard." He pointed with his fork. There was a very red, very round kidney speared on the prongs. "Damnable business this, quite damnable." He turned once more to "The Field."

General Kirk moved slowly to the sideboard and poured himself a cup of strong black coffee. His steps seemed to drag slightly on the carpet and he held his left hand in the small of his back. When he had lowered himself into a chair he reached out and took a slice of unbuttered toast.

"Just what is a damnable business, Fetherstone?" he said.

"Why, this wretched affair on the river Taff. Look at it for yerself." He pushed the paper across to him.

"Seems that Western Chemicals have put up a blasted great plant at Llanrist. Been pumping poison into the water by the ton;

fish dying all over the place. They say it gives employment and they've got to do it. Lot of stupid nonsense. I'd rather see a decent salmon than an employed Welshman any day."

"I suppose it's a sign of the times." Kirk glanced at the page. In his present state of mind he felt quite indifferent to the sufferings of others; salmon or Welshmen.

"Then all I can say is that they're damned bad times and we should try and do something about them. Soon as we get back tonight, I intend to sit down and write a stiff letter to Archibald Reade. You'll remember Archie, of course. Miserable little bounder, but he's their chairman of directors. Have to do something about it if I tell him. Damn it, I own enough shares in the concern. Quite good stock as it happens. Last dividend paid twelve and a half. If you ask me, it all comes of putting a lot of chaps from provincial universities in charge of these places. Bunch of scientists with North-Country accents who've never seen a salmon that wasn't out of a tin. Quite disgraceful." He cut himself a large slice of mutton and then looked at Kirk's modest plate.

"Here, what's that you've got old chap; dry toast? That won't take you far you know. Never heard of such a thing, just go back and help yourself to some decent grub."

"Thank you, no. Not just at the moment." Kirk looked with distaste at his friend's heaped plate.

"Quite sure, well, I suppose it's your business, but remember, we've got a stiff day in front of us." He leaned across the table and squinted at Kirk. His eye-brows were very thick and needed trimming and he looked like an ill-tempered chimpanzee.

"The moors aren't getting you down, are they? They do sometimes, with you city chaps who've spent all your lives frowsting away in stuffy little offices. Soon passes though. A couple of weeks on the heather and you won't know yerself. Get out of the way, Bessie." He pushed back his chair, kicked the Labrador to one side and began to fill a large cherry-wood pipe.

"Yes, I'm sure you're right and it's nothing to worry about of course. I'm just a little stiff and tired." Kirk's hand stole round to the small of his back. "It will pass of course, but I thought, that is

I wondered—" he glanced anxiously at his host—"if I'd better stay at home today. That is if you don't mind?"

"What's that? Not going out today? Rubbish, of course I mind. I mind very much. Why, we're beating Cold Withens today. Saved it especially for you. Best moor in the district. Always a north wind up there and the birds come over like ruddy cannon balls. Of course you must come for your own sake. I'd never forgive myself if I let you miss the Withens. Last year I got eighty-six—no eighty-seven brace and half a dozen black-cock. Now go and get some proper food into yourself. Damn near freezing on the Withens even in August. Of course if you really are feeling groggy we can fix you up with a pony, like the rest of the old crocks."

"No, no, not a pony, thanks." Kirk's heavy face took on an expression of tragic self-pity. "Just how far is it to walk?"

"How far? Depends how we go. As the crow flies or as the beggar hops." He laughed uproariously at the well worn joke. "Not far to the butts, really. We'll leave the cars at Bishop's Folly and work round by Craggy End and Lover's Lay-by. 'Bout six or seven miles, I suppose. Good stiff going, though. Put some color into you. Better than sitting about catching spies, eh?"

"Yes, yes, I suppose you're right." Kirk looked sadly at the head of a twelve pointed stag on the wall in front of him. There was an unpleasant sneering expression about its mouth and glass eyes.

"Of course you suppose so." Holt slopped more coffee into his cup and swung round angrily as the door opened.

"Well, what the blazes do you want, Glossop? How often do I have to tell you that I want no disturbances during breakfast?"

"Gent for the General, sir." Glossop had a low brow, a broken nose and few social graces. He looked rather like his master and was an ex-gamekeeper, relegated to butlering through age and infirmity.

"Damn you, Glossop. Why didn't you tell this—this gentleman that General Kirk was at breakfast and not to be disturbed. Shameful, quite shameful, calling at this hour. Hope he's not a friend of your's, old chap, but nobody seems to have any proper manners these days. Comes of free education, I shouldn't wonder. Very well, Glossop, don't just stand there, man. Get out and tell him to wait."

"One moment, Fetherstone." A slight gleam of hope was beginning to show in Kirk's tired eyes. "It might be someone I should see at once. What did he say his name was, Glossop?"

"'Oward, sir. Mister Michael 'Oward. 'Ighly important, he said it was."

"Ah, in that case perhaps I'd better go. It may be something urgent. You will excuse me a minute, won't you?" He got up and walked to the door. His step was much lighter as he followed Glossop to the library.

Michael stood by the fire-place looking at a picture of a small man in Sherlock Holmes costume, standing beside a fish. They both had identical expressions, but the fish was slightly the larger of the two. He smiled as Kirk came into the room, but his face was a little anxious.

"Good morning, sir. So sorry to barge in on you at this hour, but I wanted to catch you before you went out on the moors. The fact is I felt I needed a chat with you about this Gerda Raine business."

"That's quite all right, Mike. Very glad to see you." Kirk didn't come into the room at once. He stood by the door for a moment and then pulled it quickly open. When he was sure that Glossop had gone he shut it and took a cigar from his pocket. As soon as it started to draw properly he settled himself on the sofa. From outside there came a sudden yapping of dogs and the sound of tires on the gravel.

"Before we start to talk about the case, Mike, you'd better shut that damned window. Good, that's much better. Now, sit down and tell me all about it."

For perhaps ten minutes Michael talked and when he had finished there was a strange eager gleam in Kirk's eyes.

"Yes, it is odd isn't it. Very odd. I wonder if it is our show, though. I rather doubt it at the moment. Peter Kun and his merry men may do some unpleasant things but this doesn't seem their line of country. If it's not them then who is it? There's much more in this than a simple murder. That chap—thank you, Carlton—may be a psychopath, but he doesn't sound like one to me. Yes, it's all very interesting. So many witnesses and so many coincidences aren't there? Too many."

He leaned back in his seat staring up at the ceiling, and all trace of tiredness had gone from his face. He looked what he was, a very efficient piece of machinery.

"You know, Mike, I'd like to have a go at this, I really would. Tell me, do you think the Minechester police would let us hold a watching brief?"

"I know they'd be delighted, sir. The Chief Constable told me so himself. Since those witnesses turned up and identified Carlton they don't know where they are. They don't want to call in the Yard but if they can't crack it in three days they're going to."

"Are they indeed. Three days, I wonder. I wonder if you and I and Penny could make it in three days. I think we might, you know." There was a curious eager expression on his face. "Yes, I think we just might."

"But, sir, that's quite out of the question. What about your holiday? You can't possibly cut it short now. Why, you've been looking forward to it for weeks, talking about it all the time."

"Yes, I have, haven't I?" He looked at the door and then leaned forward to Michael. "Now listen to me, son. I've got something to tell you and if you breathe a word about it, I'll have you out of the department on your ear." Once more there came the quick nervous glance to the door.

"This isn't a holiday and I'd give six months of my life to cut it short. It's just like hard labor. All day and every day out on those blasted moors. More than a sweet-tempered mule could stand. My feet hurt, my chest hurts and I'm pretty certain I've broken my back. I can't even enjoy these any more." He looked sadly at the stump of his cigar.

"Bored as well, bored stiff. When these people aren't trying to kill animals they talk about 'em; nothing but yatter, yatter all the time about birds, guns and evil-smelling dogs. I just can't stand any more of it, Mike." He looked towards the window where a shooting brake was unloading a noisy party of large men and lean, hard-faced women.

"If I had the nerve I'd hook it back to town but that's impossible. I've talked about this—this holiday for so long that I'd be the laughing stock of the office if I broke it off now. No, this Minechester business sounds as if it might be the let-out. Interesting too, very interesting indeed." There was a slight smile on his face but it was broken off abruptly as the door burst open and his host strode into the room.

"Ah, there you are, old chap. Time to get started. Aren't you going to introduce me to yer friend?"

"Er, yes, of course. This is Michael Howard, my assistant. I'm afraid he has brought me some rather bad news."

"How are you, Howard. Bad news, eh?" Holt extended a gnarled hand. "Sorry about that, but as you're here you'd better join us. The place is crawling with birds and I can fix you up with a gun and some proper togs." He looked with distaste at Michael's urban suit. "Let you have Edith Summerskill as well."

"Edith Summerskill, sir!" Michael raised his eyebrows slightly.

"Yes, Dr. Edith Summerskill, to give her her full title. One of the best Cocker bitches I've ever had. Call all me dogs after Radical politicians. I was going to keep her in as she's due to be salt soon, but as you're a friend of Kirk's, we'll take a chance on it."

Very politely Michael declined this elderly Nimrod's offer.

"Sorry, sir. I really would love to join you, but I'm afraid it's out of the question. I have brought bad news, you see, and I have to ask the General to come back with me. The fact is that we've run into a spot of bad trouble and without him I doubt if we can get out of it." He turned sadly to Kirk. "The Minister himself was quite adamant about it, sir."

"But damnation." Clumber-Holt's face took on a dark purple flush. "This is abominable. Who is this Minister of yours? Yes, Canrose ain't it? Ruddy lowland Scotsman. Immoral fellow too. Married Judith Farquhar, didn't he? One of the best women I've ever seen after hounds, and he had the impertinence to divorce her on some trumped up charge of persistent cruelty. Wretched little coward. Now you just get on to the phone to him, old chap and tell the brute where he gets off."

Very slowly Kirk shook his head and his face took on a sad and rather noble expression. All at once Michael was reminded of an early Victorian lithograph he had seen in his youth. It had shown a soldier standing at a cross-roads surrounded by his weeping family. One path led home towards an ivy-covered cottage and the other to the smoke of the battle-field. The man's expression had been very like Kirk's and the caption below had read; "Twixt love and duty."

"No, I'm sorry, Fetherstone, but in my job, self just doesn't count. I'm sure you understand."

"Do I? Oh, yes, I suppose I do." Holt scowled at him for a moment and then his face brightened.

"Tell you what we'll do. I'll save Wet Hollow for you. You get off and finish this business as soon as you can. Find the chap you're after, stand him up in front of a wall and then come straight back and we'll have a day in the Hollow. Always good sport there, one of the hardest shoots in the district." He started as a motor horn sounded from the drive.

"Well, I'm afraid I must go now, old chap. Can't keep the fellows waiting if you're not joining us. Now remember, just you get back as soon as you can and we'll have that day in the Hollow. Goodbye for the time being."

"Goodbye, Fetherstone and thank you. I'll look forward to it." Kirk watched him strut out of the door then the martyred expression lifted and his face burst into a grin.

"Thanks, Mike," he said. "Thanks, you did very well. Bah, Wet Hollow. Now, just give me five minutes to collect my things and I'll be with you. Got a car outside? Good, see you there then." He turned away and in spite of a slight limp his step was almost boyish.

Once the police car that Hailstone had loaned him turned out of the gates of Nantwood Lodge, Michael saw that his chief had quite returned to his normal self. For a moment or two he joked and chatted with Penny then turned to the job in hand.

"Right, let's get down to it, shall we? Michael has given me a short verbal account of this business, my dear, but I suppose you've got some notes in writing. Good, I can never really picture anything unless I see it in front of me. Thank you." He took the transcript from Penny and started to read as the car hit a bad patch of road.

"Constable, I wonder if you would do me a favor?" He leaned forward and tapped the uniformed driver on the shoulder. "I wonder if for the next ten minutes you could cease to imagine you are Stirling Moss hurling the mighty Mercedes around Silverstone Circuit, and become a poverty stricken private chauffeur. You have six children and an ailing wife to support and are employed by a nervous dowager who will sack you without references at the merest suspicion of a jolt. Very many thanks, Constable."

He stretched back against the cushions and for a while there was silence in the car, broken only by the whine of the tires and the rustle of paper as he turned the pages. They were almost in the Minechester suburbs when at last he handed the notes back to Penny.

"Thank you, my dear. A very nice and clear account. Michael's a lucky chap. Now, let's talk about it. Tell me, Mike. What do you think is the oddest thing about this business?"

"I don't know, sir, but I think the time. Everybody seems so certain about the time. She comes into the bar at such and such a time, she leaves at such and such a time. People see her watch and hear the clock and are prepared to swear to it. She gets off the bus at ten to ten and we can be almost sure that she was killed dead on the hour. It's almost as if everybody was watching a time-table."

"Yes, isn't it. Time, people and coincidence. Lots of people." He looked out of the window at the growing town. "People who are there just when they can see something that is important. It's all very neat, isn't it? A place for everything and everything in its place.

"Yes, lots of people and some of them are wrong. Gerda, for instance. A very sharp, clever little girl, who is able to get the better of the Russians and ourselves but unable to stop somebody filling her up with dope. A respectable girl, who dresses herself up like a tart and goes to the pub with a woman of a certain type whom nobody recognizes. And in that pub, just where he is wanted, in the right place at the right time, she meets Carlton. Carlton, who bears a grudge against loose women because of his father; Carlton who has never been in that bar before and has only the money for one drink; Carlton who takes the very seat on the bus where he is bound to be noticed; Carlton who would be the obvious suspect if just at the right time two impeccable witnesses were not taking their little white terrier for a walk and see him leave the girl."

"And you think, sir—"

"I don't think anything yet, Mike, I don't have to. I've got two full days before I need to start thinking, so at the moment I just wonder. In those days I want to know a great deal about a great many people. As soon as I've got a room at your hotel and changed into some proper clothes I intend to call on your pal Captain Thunderstorm and prepare a little visiting list. Gerda Raine was in this town about a month. I want to know why she came here in the first place and what she was like while she was with this Mrs. Brett and the lodging house she went to afterwards. I want to speak to everybody who knew her and, if I'm lucky, the last person I speak to will be the killer.

"At the moment I don't like this affair at all. It's all too well ordered for my money. There may be a criminal lunatic in the background but if there is, he's a jolly efficient one. Good God! Is this it?" He broke off as the car slid to a halt and frowned at the dark pile of the "Three Mitres Hotel."

"Blimey, Mike, you certainly pick 'em don't you. Tell me, where did you take your degree? I see, Durham. That may account for it. As my old pal Fetherstone Holt would say, it all comes of putting chaps from provincial universities in charge."

He flung open the door, bawled for a porter and strode up the steep, pretentious steps. Just at the top, he turned and looked at them.

"You know, we've used the word coincidence quite a lot this morning. Too many coincidences. We may be right but I'm beginning to wonder if it's not the wrong word and wants changing to another one beginning with 'C'. Yes, Mike. Not coincidence; just conspiracy."

He marched on into the hall and as she looked at his strong, self-confident back Penny felt a slight feeling of pity for the killer of Gerda Raine.

CHAPTER FIVE

Let him go or let him tarry, let him sink or let him swim.
He doesn't care for me and I don't care for him—

The record was worn and harsh but the power was there and the jukebox of the "Castle Inn" gave it the full treatment. Kirk grinned through the almost overpowering atmosphere and ordered another round of drinks. He wore a tight, rather oversmart suit and a carnation drooped in his buttonhole. He had the sad, jolly air of an old but still serviceable roué. The few male customers didn't like the look of him, but the women at the bar crowded round him, laughing at his jokes and answering his innocent questions freely. Every time he asked for drinks their eyes kept flicking towards the thick green lips of his wallet.

"And as you say, my dear lady, neither you nor any of your charming friends had seen either of them before. Odd that, very odd. A most terrible business in every way. The real tragedy is that I have such little confidence in our friends the police. Exactly, how right you are; they spend far too much time hounding perfectly respectable citizens to give real criminals the least attention. Cheers." He lifted the slightly cracked glass to his lips, swept a bland smile round the counter and all the time as he drank and talked and listened his keen mind was split and waiting.

This was where it began. Four nights ago, Gerda Raine had sat just where he was sitting; a little blonde girl with clothes that weren't her clothes and things in her bag that weren't hers either. On this very seat she had sat, swaying towards her companion as the drug took control while her watch lay flat on the counter or swung at her side for everyone to see it was right. And just behind her there had been Carlton; James Carlton with two shillings in his pocket which he had spent on beer because the pub was bright and he liked music. The same music perhaps that was cutting the atmosphere at the moment.

Let him go to his old mother who I hope he will enjoy—

And Carlton had a mother; he had a mother whose husband had left her for a girl two years after he was born. Carlton who at a word of command had got up from his table and followed the old tart out to the bus stop with twopence in his pocket and his empty restless hands. Carlton who was now completely in the clear because he had two witnesses who had seen him just at the right time and in the right place.

For I'm going to marry a far nicer boy.

Yes, not Carlton but another boy; a far cleverer boy than Carlton. Somebody from the bar perhaps, who had heard what the old woman said and followed the bus to the river. Somebody who had been there before and waited at the top of the steps, knowing that Carlton might get frightened and go away, leaving a little drugged girl behind him. Somebody who knew a great deal about time and place.

He considered the two witnesses he had seen that afternoon. Both reliable men whose statements had to be accepted. Mr. Stokes, tall and lean, a foreman welder in the shipyards. Mr. Kerr, large and red-faced, a shopkeeper, a local magistrate and a great eater of meat. Two friends who always took the same walk together at the same time; along the quay-side and then up the steps because it was good exercise and Kerr's old terrier was getting fat. Kirk pictured them reaching the top of those steps, seeing the girl leaning against the wall and Carlton walking away from them and now and again turning to see if they were following. Odd, they would think, but not their business. It was an unpleasant part of the town and the girl was of a certain type and plainly drunk, so they had carried on with their walk and forgotten about it till they had heard the police ask for help on the radio.

He imagined the sound of their footsteps dying away on the cobbles and the girl left alone by the wall; her mind still dim with the drug perhaps, but starting to clear a little as she took in her surroundings. The tall houses waiting for demolition, the loom of the bridges and the glint of water at the bottom of the steps. Then at last up the steps—someone.

He looked at his watch, looked up at the clock above the bar and took a pound note from his wallet.

"Landlord, I wonder if you would be kind enough to give these ladies what they require. No, I fear that this time I cannot have the pleasure of joining them. A friend to be met and a train to be caught." He stood up and bowed deeply.

"Dear ladies, this has been a very great pleasure. I do hope we will meet again." He turned and walked through the room with its atmosphere of old decayed gaiety, into the night.

And it was already night. Though it was just nine thirty on an August evening it was quite dark. A thin mist had drifted in from the river and was beginning to form little hanging spirals over the town; an early to bed town. As it had been on that other evening, the bus was almost empty. Kirk sat on the back seat where Gerda Raine had sat and watched the conductor making up his log for the final journey. Beyond him through the steaming glass he could see lighted shop windows with nobody in front of them, and here and there an odd figure, late from the office, hurrying home before the fog thickened. He thought of Carlton obediently handing out the three fares that the old woman had given him, watching her get off at the cinema and going on alone with the girl to the place where she was to be met. He could see it all quite clearly and far back in his old, efficient mind, the first pieces of the puzzle were beginning to fit together.

"Terminus, sir. This is where we finish." The conductor pushed his log book and ticket machine into a metal box and started to light a cigarette.

"Thank you." Kirk stood up and moved out onto the platform. "I expect you manage to make pretty good time on this last run."

"Well, we try to, sir." The man grinned at him. "It's always dead slack and we could knock off five minutes if we had the chance. Trouble is that the inspector has a fit if we get to the garage early so it's always dead on ten to when we get here. Goodnight, sir."

"Goodnight to you." Kirk stepped off the bus and turned up his collar. The mist was quite thick now, with a few drops of rain in it. Already it blanketed the tower of the the Gothic cathedral and the line of tall warehouses. Across the street by the cul-de-sac he could see the waiting police car. Its lights had an oddly greenish tinge.

"Hullo, General, dead on time." Inspector Ellis got out of the car and held the door open for Penny and Michael. "Did you learn anything from your little tour of reconstruction?"

"No, nothing that matters as yet, but then you see, I didn't expect to. Just wanted to get the feel of things, the atmosphere of the murder if you like. I think I'm beginning to and it's not very pleasant."

"No, sir, but murder never is. In particular this kind of murder." The policeman looked doubtfully at him for a moment. "Well this is the place. They got off the bus just as you did and he took her down here. It's just a dead end for traffic, only the steps to the river run out of it."

"I see." Kirk looked around him at the dark unlighted houses. Far above his head there lay the gigantic loom of the railway bridge, oddly distorted in the fog, while somewhere down river a ship's siren bellowed three times.

"I think you told me that all this area is going to come down."

"Quite right, sir. It's all due for demolition and rebuilding as soon as the council can raise the money. Pity in a way. Fine old houses some of these, though they've mostly gone to rack and ruin. Look at this one for instance." He shone his torch to a door way to the right. It had a handsome stone arch with a carved inscription above the frame.

"The story is that this house used to belong to a French priest; a refugee from the revolution. Can you read the first line of the writing, sir? It says *Merci Beaucoup*, which means thank you very much. I expect it was a compliment to the person who gave him the house."

"And thank you very much for telling me, Inspector. Strangely enough, even I knew the translation of *merci beaucoup*." He squinted at the words below it. "As you seem to be so well informed, perhaps you can tell me what the rest of the message means?"

"That I can't tell you, sir. Looks like Greek to me."

"And there I'm afraid you're wrong. Not Greek, Latin. Rather clumsy Latin too. Dog Latin, they'd call it. Medieval Monk Latin. Strange for anybody to use it as late as the eighteenth century. Hold your torch a little lower. Yes. *'Alberti Minimi Sacris Laus et Gloria Magistri.'* That would roughly say, All praise to the master and the mysteries of Albert the Little. I wonder who this Mr. Albertus may have been? Still, not really our business, is it?"

"No, sir, of course not. Shall we go on down then?"

"By all means, coming children?" Kirk smiled at Penny and Michael and started to follow Ellis down the alley. Their feet sounded dull and lifeless in the thick air.

"Here are the steps, sir. I'd take them a bit easy if I were you. They're very steep and not in the best of repair. There's a rail by the side there which might help you a bit."

"Thank you." Kirk reached out his hand and took it. The iron was bloated with rust and felt soft and unpleasant to the touch, like something that had died a long time ago under water. Far above them the bridge began to sing and vibrate as a train pulled slowly to the south. The lighted windows and the glow of the locomotive looked warm and comforting as they passed over the dark town.

"Nine fifty-five to London, sir. I expect you wish you were on it."

"Yes, in a way I do, Inspector, in a way. Ah, here we are." The steps turned a corner and gave way to a concrete slope. In front of them there was a glint of water; a grey sump separated from the river by a wooden mole.

"Yes, this is it. We're almost dead on time too, sir. Yes." He listened as the cathedral clock began to strike the hour. "We found the body just there, about five yards from the quay."

For a moment the four of them stood still, looking at the water. Then Kirk heard a long sigh from Penny.

"Oh, Mike," she said. "Poor girl. I know that when she was alive I hated her and now she's dead it's not supposed to matter. But poor little girl. What a dreadful place to die in."

"Yes, what a place." Kirk's eyes followed the beam of the torch across the sump with its grey scum floating on the surface by the mole, the broken bottles and the rusty moorings and the oil film drifting in from the river, and he felt cold because it was what he expected; exactly what he expected. All the time in the bar, on the bus, walking down the steps, he had known that it would be like this. It had to be like this. There was no other place that would do. No other possible end to the story.

"Just how much can you hate a person," he thought. "Just how much hatred can there be that needs to do this to her. You fill her up with dope and dress and disguise her as a tart and give her to a half-wit to take to the killer. But even that is not enough for you. The place of death must be right as well. The final humiliation. The grave among the scum, the floating bottles, the oil film and the—" there was a dull sound in front of him and he felt Penny stiffen. "Yes, and the rats as well."

He looked out across the river to a big cluster of lights where a freighter was unloading on the far bank. There was no chance of reading the letters on her stern or the limp flag at the mast, but he didn't need to. He had already checked her identity from the shipping lists. Her name was the "Rosa Luxemburg" and her flag bore the bright bars of the East German People's Republic. For quite a long time he looked at her and then he turned to Ellis.

"Now, Inspector, let's think about the time factor for a moment. We have the evidence of a number of witnesses and the broken watch which makes it pretty certain that she was killed just on ten o'clock. That's right, isn't it?"

"Quite right, sir, but what of it?" Ellis' tone was slightly impatient and he was beginning to think this visit of Kirk's was becoming an intolerable nuisance. He longed to get back to his warm car, the police station and the mug of scalding tea which would be waiting for him there.

"I don't know yet, possibly nothing, but I want to be sure. There's a little experiment I want to try before I know if it means anything. Firstly, I want you to remember something. Those two men who saw Carlton. Yes, Kerr and Stokes. Think what they said. All the time they were coming up the steps the dog kept turning and pulling on the lead. Why do you think he would do that, Inspector?"

"Obvious, sir. They were being followed by somebody and the dog sensed it. That's the fact on which we base our present theory. Somebody came up the steps behind them and took the girl down; the real killer in fact, General."

"So, that's what you think is it? Quite an interesting notion, but I wonder if it will hold water. Remember what else those men said. They both agreed that they looked back at the girl just before they turned out into the main road. She was still leaning against the wall and was quite still. Then they looked up at the cathedral clock and the time was six minutes to ten. Six minutes, old boy. Six minutes for someone to get her down here, kill her, mutilate the body, and throw her into the water. I wonder if it could be done?" He looked thoughtfully at the flight of steps and then turned to Penny.

"Just how much do you weigh, my dear. Thank you. A hundred and thirty pounds. Better watch it. A little heavier than Gerda but I'll allow for that. Now, I want to try a little experiment. I want you and Michael to go up the first fifty of these steps. You will play the part of the victim. You are full of dope and will be quite limp and helpless. Right, Mike, take her up those fifty steps and then try to get her down. Use any method you like, but get her down as quickly as you can." He watched them walk up the stairs, then took out his watch and set the stop lever.

"Are you ready up there? Right, start now."

They made slow progress down. The steps were worn and chipped and polished by generations. Penny held herself quite limp and from time to time Michael slipped and stumbled under her weight and leaned against the wall. He was breathing quickly when at last he reached the water's edge.

"Good, a very convincing performance I should say. Don't you agree, Inspector? I was thinking of timing the killing too, but I don't think it will be necessary now. Let's see what it tells us." He held his watch under the torch.

"Yes, it has taken Mr. Howard a little under two minutes. Though Mrs. Wise is heavier than the dead girl, he wasn't worried about noise as the real killer would have been. There are two hundred steps, I understand, so we must allow eight minutes to get her down to the water. Then our pal has to stab her nine times, batter her face in with the piece of scrap-iron he found lying about and throw her in the water. Say ten minutes at the very outside. But you haven't got ten minutes, have you, old man?" He turned a crooked smile on Ellis. "Only six, it seems that your theory is a little ambitious."

For a moment Ellis didn't answer him. His lips moved slightly as he made his calculations and there was a terrible bewilderment in his eyes.

"But this can't be right," he said at last. "There must be an explanation somewhere. We know the times are right. We've got the witnesses, the medical evidence, the watch. She was at the top of the steps at six minutes to and she died on the hour. And somewhere we're wrong because it's just not humanly possible.

"Yes, somewhere we're wrong." Kirk looked past him towards the lights of the "Rosa Luxemburg." She was quite low in the water now, and there was a line of trucks at her side. If they got the ballast in quickly she would sail on the morning tide. He scowled at her and pulled his coat more tightly around him.

"Yes, somewhere we're wrong; very wrong. By all accounts there wasn't a murder at all. There was though, because you've got a body in your morgue to prove it. Very, very odd." He began to walk towards the steps and then turned and looked at Ellis.

"What was it you said just now? Yes, not humanly possible. I wonder if that's where we're wrong. Not humanly possible." Once more came the slow smile.

"Yes, I wonder if that might be our mistake. Because of the time factor it does not seem humanly possible. I wonder if that's it. Humanly. Perhaps it wasn't. Perhaps it wasn't a he or a she who took Gerda down the steps but just an It?"

He pulled down his hat and walked briskly forward.

CHAPTER SIX

Number 34 Popes Grove was quite definitely "U" and in very much the best part of the town. It had white gates, a double garage and a rock-garden that looked like something out of a seedsman's catalogue. It was a very nice example of expensive suburbia. Across the road and away from it, lawns ran down to a park with an ornamental lake surrounded by rose bushes.

Kirk walked slowly up the path to the front door. He had put away his clothes of the night before and looked very respectable in dark grey serge. Just before he pressed the gleaming bell-push he leaned over towards Penny.

"Now, remember, girl. As I told you before, I don't imagine we'll learn much here, but we can't be sure and people always talk better on their own. If we get the opportunity of splitting them, we'll do so. I'll take the mother and you concentrate on the son. Give him the full treatment. Understand?" His hand came down on the bell and from the back of the house he heard a soft melodious chime.

From outside the house they had both imagined that the door would be opened by an over-smart maid in musical comedy uniform. They were wrong; it was a man. He was a tall, fair man and he looked beautiful with crinkly hair and a very white smile. He wore a blue blazer with a crest and fawn slacks. His scarf had little golden lions on it and they seemed to dance in the sunlight. He made a dashing picture as he stood on the step.

"Good afternoon, sir and—madam." His smile lapped around Penny like a caress. "And what can I have the pleasure of doing for you?"

"Good afternoon." Kirk took off his hat and gave the vision a courteous nod. "I wonder if Mrs. Brett could spare us a moment of her time?"

"Oh, dear. Mrs. Brett, not Mister. Pity. I was hoping that it was myself you were wanting to see." Once more his eyes touched Penny. She was wearing a sack-line dress but somehow managed to make it look full.

"Do come in though. I really don't know when my mother will be back, but I don't expect she'll be too long." He stood back and motioned them into a very light hall that smelt slightly of lavender. There were good modern reproductions on the walls and the furniture was mainly white wood and chrome steel. It was all well done and had cost a great deal of money.

The man pulled back a curtain on the right and led them into a room that was like the hall only more so. It had Pueblo rugs on the floor and a lot of book-cases. For a second Penny glanced at the titles. They were all of the same type; modern first editions, collectors' pieces, which could never be read for fear of damaging the dust jackets and they had an oddly sterile look.

"Please sit down won't you. I'm Mrs. Brett's son." He moved across the room and brought over a cedar-wood box divided into two compartments.

"Cigarette? We have good Turkish, mine, and poor Virginian, Mother's."

"Thank you, not just at the moment." Kirk shook his head and watched Penny take a poor Virginian.

"Perhaps we'd better introduce ourselves. My name is Kirk and this is Mrs. Wise, my secretary. Let me give you a card."

"Thank you, Mr. Kirk." Brett took the card and glanced at it briefly; not for one moment did his studied expression alter.

"But how intriguing. General Charles Kirk. You know I don't think that I've ever met a full general." He lowered himself onto a tapestry covered stool. "Can you tell me what you want to see my mother about, or is it top secret?"

"Not a bit of it, Mr. Brett. Probably you'll be able to help us as much as she can. The fact is that I'm not really a general now.

That card is just an old man's vanity; retired long ago. Now I hold a pretty minor desk job with the Immigration Department and they've sent me up here to make a few inquiries about Gerda Raine."

"Gerda Raine?" For the first time he looked slightly bewildered. "Sorry, but the name just doesn't ring a bell."

"My fault, Mr. Brett. You would have known her as Gladys Reeves."

"Oh, poor Gladys. How stupid of me. I should have known she was really called something like that. She had one of the most ghastly German accents I've ever heard. Poor girl. What can I tell you about her, Inspector—oh dear." He broke off and blushed slightly. "Please forgive me. General, of course. We've had so many policemen about here of late that I'm getting mixed. What about Gladys? You're not going to tell me she was some kind of spy, are you?"

"Good heavens, no; nothing like that. All a lot of nonsense, really, but my superiors seem to feel we ought to look into the case. The fact is that we know very little about the girl's movements since she came to this country about two years ago and we've got to get out some kind of report, independent of the police, just in case her relatives in Germany start asking questions. Very annoying these things, Mr. Brett, they make lots of quite needless work and they never really resolve anything." He shook his head sadly.

"I see, bad luck." Brett got up and crossed to a cupboard at the back of the room. It was chrome steel and glass and looked like part of an operating theatre.

"I'm afraid I can tell you very little about her, but all the same let me get you a cocktail. I'm supposed to be rather good at them." He jiggered with ice and bottles for a moment and then brought over three glasses.

He hadn't been boasting when he said he was good. At the first sip Kirk knew that this was one of the best dry Martinis he had ever tasted. Since he had come into the house he had been itching to kick Brett, but now he looked at him with something slightly like respect.

"Thank you," he said, "this is really excellent. No, I don't suppose you can tell us very much. I doubt if anyone can. I think that she was just a silly girl who probably got into bad company. She came to your mother in answer to an advertisement I understand?"

"Yes, I think that's right. We put a line in the local rag and she turned up. As far as I can remember she had no references and merely said she had been working in London and wanted a change. As she at least looked clean, Mother took her on."

"I see. And she only stayed with you for about two weeks I think. Did she give any reason for leaving? Any new friends for instance who might have persuaded her to go? What sort of impression did you get of her, Mr. Brett?"

"No, I don't know why she left." Brett shook his beautifully barbered head. "She just said she was bored and wanted a change. Couldn't stand Minechester probably, and I can't say I blame her. As to what she was like, I'm not sure. To tell you the truth, I didn't pay a lot of attention. She was quite a pretty little thing in a common sort of way, and she seemed good at her work. At least I never heard my mother complain and she kept my books decently dusted." His limp hand swept the volumes of M.P. Shiel, Madox Ford and Frederick Corvo. As the sunlight caught his hand, Penny noticed that the nails had a thin film of polish.

"Friends, no. Definitely no. I don't think she had any letters and she hardly went out at all. She had her own key but always seemed to be in by ten. As a matter of fact I think she was slightly attracted to yours truly." Once more came the flashing glance towards Penny.

"I'm in the house a great deal in connection with my work and she used to make excuses to get into my study. Rather embarrassing at times. You know how it is, General?"

"No, I'm afraid I'm a little too old to either know or even remember." Kirk beamed at him. "What is your work if it's not impertinent to ask?"

"Of course you may ask, though as a military man, I imagine it's hardly in your line. I'm a creative writer."

"Really, but how very interesting. I'd like to read some of your work. Who are your publishers?" As he spoke Penny was suddenly reminded of a big cat creeping towards its prey.

"Alas, at the moment, Nemo. Several of the better firms are interested of course, but there are limits to what one will do, and they all suggest quite impossible alterations. When I think of the arrogance of the puffed-up school children who control these places I begin to despair for British letters. One day, of course, I shall break through, but till then I just work."

A curious expression came into his eyes and as he looked at that handsome, somehow unhandsome face, all Kirk's hostility died and he felt only sadness and compassion. Terrible compassion, for the man believed it. Under the trick hair-do, the blazer, the forced manner and the lion scarf he believed he was a genius and it was all that held him together.

"Of course, you will, Mr. Brett," he said, and his voice was very gentle. "And when you do I shall take great pleasure in reading your first published work." He broke off and stood up as the door opened behind him.

In one way the woman was like her son. She was tall and straight and blonde and rather beautiful, but there the resemblance ended; for she was strong as well. She was terribly strong. As he introduced himself, and took her hand, he felt a little of her strength in her gloved handshake.

"How do you do, General Kirk and—thank you, Mrs. Wise. I hope my son has been looking after you. Ah, I see he has." She smiled at the glasses.

"Now, what can I do for you? Oh that wretched business about poor Gladys again. I thought we would have finished with that when the police left yesterday. Besides, I know very little about her. She was only in my service for two weeks and I never even knew her proper name or heard from her after she left. Still, if there's anything you want to ask me, I am at your disposal."

Very patiently she listened to Kirk's false statement of his occupation and tried to answer his questions. She told him nothing. Gerda Raine had come in answer to an advertisement, she had done her work and gone out rarely, she seemed to have no friends.

At the end of two weeks she had left without even a forwarding address. When Mrs. Brett had finished, Kirk thanked her and stood up.

"Thank you very much, madam. That seems to be the lot then. Just one more thing before I leave you in peace. I wonder if I might take a look at the girl's room. I understand that the police have got all her things from the boarding house, but I'd like to see it. It might give me a sense of her—how shall I put it—atmosphere."

"Of course you may, General, if you think it will help. She took everything with her, but you're most welcome to look round. My son will entertain Mrs. Wise while we're gone." She turned to the door, waited for him to open it for her and led him across the hall to the stairs.

The maid's room was under the roof at the end of a short third staircase and it was quite different from the rest of the house. It wasn't bright or gleaming with steel or polish and it could hardly be called a room at all. It had an iron bed, a battered chest with open drawers and a small wardrobe, with a cracked glass. It was about ten feet square and the slope of the ceiling almost touched his head. There was only one thing in it that could even vaguely be called decorative. Just in front of the bed there was a roughly carved human figure in amber wood. Although crude it had been beautifully done and the wood seemed to grow with a life of its own. It wasn't pleasant though; the face was quite blank and without human expression. It was death, negation, the finish of the flesh and there was something wrong with the rest of the body.

"May I?" Kirk stooped beneath the eaves and looked at it. "What is it, Mrs. Brett? Is it old?"

"No, I don't think so, General. Quite modern, I understand, though I know very little about it. This century at least. It was put away in the lumber room when Gladys saw it. She asked me if she could have it in her room. Personally I find it quite repulsive, but there's no accounting for taste, I suppose." She shrugged her rather beautiful shoulders. "Have you any idea what it means?"

"No, not really, but it seems to ring a bell somehow." He ran the tip of his finger across the rough forehead. "There is obviously some Negroid influence but a lot more as well. Where did you get it?"

"My dear man, it has nothing to do with me. It was my husband's. He was a medical missionary and he traveled a great deal. He was always collecting things like that. I'm afraid I threw most of them away. Except that it's comparatively modern, I know nothing about it." She took a cigarette from her bag and lit it. As he looked at her face in the glow of the flame he knew quite definitely that she was lying.

"I see." He turned from the carving and smiled at her. "You know, I thought your name reminded me of something. Haven't I heard of your husband? Yes, Dr. Brett, I'm sure I remember something about him."

She shook her head and smiled back at him. "That's most unlikely, General Kirk. My husband did nothing very remarkable with his life. He just traveled, practiced medicine, preached the gospels and—died." There was a slight pause between the words.

"Now, is there anything more I can do for you? Please be as quick as you can. I'm a very busy woman these days."

"Of course. There's just one thing really. I think you told Inspector Ellis that you weren't really surprised when you heard that the girl had been killed. Why was that, Mrs. Brett? Was it that you felt she might have been frightened of someone?"

"Oh dear no. She wasn't frightened." The shake of the head was quite emphatic. "Gladys—sorry, Gerda—wasn't frightened of anything. I said what I did to the police because I felt it to be true. You may not understand this, but to me she seemed a typical example of the murderee."

"Sorry, I'm not with you. Just how do you mean?"

"In every way. By murderee, I mean the kind of person who asks to be murdered. I even felt it myself you know. Every time I spoke to her I felt like it. Please don't misunderstand me. She never did anything to cause it, she was always most correct; obeyed orders to the letter but it was still there. Almost as if she were saying; 'Very well, I shall do it this time, but some day our roles will be reversed and then—God help you.'"

"Yes, I think I do understand." Kirk's mind slipped back over the years and he was in his office with a little pert, rather lovely face in front of him and a voice saying: No protection, thank you. Just the passport that you were *ordered* to give me.

"Yes, I understand," he said. "And your son, do you think he felt that too?"

"Peter? Good heavens, no. The poor boy is so wrapped up in his work that he hardly notices anything. Besides, I rather doubt if she would have been quite the same with a young man."

"Possibly you're right." Kirk was inclined to doubt it. To him there seemed nothing very young or manly about Peter Brett. "Tell me, if you felt so strongly, why didn't you sack her?"

"Sack her, indeed! My dear man, it's quite easy to see you're a bachelor and probably live in some well-run club or hotel. I said that she made me feel like killing her at times, but that doesn't mean to say I wanted to lose a perfectly good servant. No, I was honestly very sorry to see her go."

"And she gave no reason for leaving?"

"None at all. She merely said she wanted a change. Now is there anything else?" She glanced at the platinum watch. Like all her possessions except the contents of this one room it was very expensive. "As I told you, I'm a busy woman. That's not a way of getting rid of you, but quite true. In these days of high taxation I need a part-time job and as I'm quite good at figures I help a firm of accountants. At the moment there are five sets of books waiting for me."

"No, nothing else for the time being, Mrs. Brett, and thank you so much for your help." Kirk gave a final glance at the strange figure on the wall and then followed her out of the room. At the landing she paused and held out her hand.

"Will you forgive me if I don't come down, General? My office is on this floor and Peter will show you out. Goodbye. I do hope we may meet again under happier circumstances."

"Goodbye, Mrs. Brett." Kirk watched her go into a room at the end of the landing and shut the door behind her. He began to walk toward the stairs and then paused.

Just in front of him there was another room. The door was ajar and inside he could see a very nice rose-wood desk with a white typewriter and a manuscript beside it. He looked behind him and then walked in and turned over the typescript. It was an expert job with vellum covers and the title page was in red. It looked very efficient.

"The Day of the Wanderer," he read, "90,000 words. A Modern Fantasy by Peter Brett 34 Popes Grove Minechester 7. Part I. The Birth of the Fire by Peter Brett 34 Popes Grove Minechester 7. If found return at once to Peter Brett 34 Popes Grove Minechester 7."

He grinned. Whoever was given this manuscript to check would remember the name and address. He sat down and started to read.

His action came purely from curiosity and he expected nothing except its satisfaction, yet at the third line he stiffened. He bent forward over the papers and he was quite unworried at the thought of discovery and completely fascinated by what he read; for it was good, it was terribly good. By the time he reached the end of the second page he knew that what he had before him was the real thing; the true authentic work of the craftsman. He felt a great sense of awe and humility as he turned the third page.

Suddenly he stopped. He looked for a long time at a passage and there was bewilderment in his eyes, then he turned back to the opening page and his expression changed from awe to sadness; great sadness. After he had read five more lines, he closed the book, pushed back his chair and stood up. He knew quite clearly that his first judgment was correct. The book was good but it was quite wrong; as wrong as the body of the little wooden statue over the maid's bed. The vellum covers, the neat typing, the changed phrases and the altered names were all right. Everything else was false and meaningless and it had nothing to do with Peter Brett. It was a work of art of a very strange kind and Peter Brett had sat down at his white typewriter and faithfully copied it from the writings of that odd genius who took the name of Father Rolfe, Frederick Baron Corvo.

He walked quickly down the stairs, growled at Penny to follow him and with a curt nod to Brett, walked out to the waiting car.

Not till they had turned out of the prosperous suburb did he speak.

"Well, my dear, how did you get on? Find out anything from our blue-eyed boy?"

"Not really, General, except that before long he's going to fill the Thames full of petrol and throw a match at it. Pretty fast worker though, tried to make a pass at me. Asked me to have dinner with him as well."

"The devil he did. And did you feel any urge to accept?"

"You know, I did in a way. He was quite amusing at times and he knows how to flatter a girl, which is a change after Mike. Still I'm not sure." She frowned for a moment. "You see, there was something about him I didn't understand. All the time he was talking to me I had the feeling that he wasn't there at all, wasn't a real person. All his jokes, his conceits, his nice manners, seemed as if they were part of a mask which was trying to hide something else. And you know, the odd thing was that I didn't feel there was anything at all to hide. I'm afraid that must seem very silly to you."

"No, Penny, it's not silly, not silly at all and I think I know what you mean. There was nothing to hide; nothing except the mask. It's like we used to say in Daddy's Big War, 'Seven Eights of Nine Tenths of "F" all,' and it's very sad."

For a moment Kirk's two fingers brushed against her arm and he seemed to draw a little strength from the feel of her strong young body. Then he looked out at the town.

It was still bright sunlight but somehow it looked worse in the sun, with every brick of every dark building gaunt and staring and slightly indecent, like old street-walkers robbed of their make-up. Suddenly, because he felt like it, he leaned forward and bawled at the driver.

"Come on, Mike Hawthorn, get your flat foot down," he said, and the driver who understood him now grinned back. He scowled at him through the mirror and stretched on the cushions and closed his eyes.

"Yes," he thought, "she's right because it is silly. That's the only word that fits, just silly. The whore who isn't a whore, but quite respectable. The man sitting at the typewriter copying out Corvo while his mother adds up accounts. The other man taking the girl to the river on his one pint of bitter beer. All that and a statue too. A crude native carving that was wrong, all wrong." As his eyes opened, he suddenly knew just why it was wrong. It wasn't the blind head, the expression or even the sense of despair that was wrong, it was something much simpler; the stance. The limbs were wrong because they hinged backwards. Neck, groin, knees and elbows, they were broken and they hinged backwards. The thing was a cripple and it could never move the right way.

He turned towards Penny and beyond her face he saw the flat blind features of the statue. He forced his mind backwards, searching for what it reminded him of and all at once he was a boy again; an inky bored unhappy boy of thirteen, sitting in the school chapel while a missionary with a high-pitched voice spoke of the enemies of Christendom about the world.

His lips moved slowly as he remembered but the words were low and quite indistinguishable under the whine of the tires.

"I wonder," he said, "I just wonder if that old fool was right and it was something like that." He thought for a moment and then spoke to Penny.

"Listen, my dear. I'm not sure yet, but I'm getting a feeling that we're out of our depth here and need a bit of expert advice. I'm going up to town and try and get it. You and Mike keep out of mischief and I'll ring you in the morning. Now, tell that oaf in front to take us to the station."

Once more he leaned back and tried to think of the statue. It was very strange but for a moment he seemed to see that blind face smiling at him.

CHAPTER SEVEN

About an hour before Kirk had bent over Brett's copied manuscript, Michael Howard pulled a rusty bell handle in Ladysmith Road. Ladysmith Road was quite different from Popes Grove. It was a long dusty street with disused tram lines, little shops and children playing before the doors of decayed Regency houses. There were dockyards behind and from time to time he heard the rattle of a riveting machine. It was all very work-a-day and even the public houses he had passed bore industrial names; "The Locomotive," "The Steam Hammer" and "The Hydraulic Crane."

Michael leaned against the peeling paint of the door frame and waited; he was very tired and very bored. This was his fifth call that day and he was beginning to believe that the murder had never happened at all. There seemed to be no logical way in which it could have happened. Everything seemed to add together to make it completely impossible.

He considered the people he had seen. The mate of the tug first; a big, overbearing, unpleasant man, but a reliable witness who would hold to his story. He had heard a splash and a sound of somebody running; the time had been ten o'clock.

After him had come the bus conductor; very friendly and ready to help and quite definite in his theory. The girl's watch had been right by the clock on the War Memorial and he had seen them off the bus at ten minutes to the hour.

Then the two men who had seen Carlton on the steps; just as definite. The girl had been alive at six minutes to ten and Carlton had walked in front of them.

And finally, Mrs. Carlton herself. She had been very nice, very helpful. She was delighted to have her son back and chatted happily to Michael and given him tea while James sat in front of them and grinned shyly. But there, too, there was nothing to learn. James had been brought up to respect elderly women and he had taken the girl on the bus because he had been asked. He had got frightened when she scratched him and gone away, leaving her there. There was nothing more to say.

And that was that. He had seen six people; six people who seemed to have nothing to gain or lose by lying and every one of them had told him that the murder was quite impossible. Now, as he waited outside the house where Gerda Raine had spent her last weeks he was almost prepared to believe them. And that was wrong, too, for it had happened. Whatever these honest, respectable witnesses might say, it had happened, and there was a body in the morgue to prove it. He stood back from the door as footsteps sounded in the passage and a bolt was drawn back.

The human being who opened the door could have been any age. Her hair had a slightly blonde tinge, but that might have been dye. Her hands were worn and wrinkled, like an old woman's, but that might have been work. She could have been anything from fifteen to fifty and her face had a pallor that made her look as if she had never seen the sun.

"Yes," she said and there was no statement, no question or greeting in the word. It was just a word; the routine formula which went with the chore of opening the door.

"Good afternoon. Could I see Mrs. Travers, please?" Michael took off his hat and smiled at the white face, but she didn't even look at him.

"Wait," she said, "I'll see," she turned back down the passage. Her walk was oddly lifeless and automatic, as if there were invisible wires attached to her feet lifting them without any will of her own. From somewhere at the back of the house he could hear a piano playing one of Chopin's Nocturnes. The music was very correct, very accomplished but somehow, like the woman's walk, quite without life or feeling.

"Good afternoon. My servant tells me that you wish to see me." Mrs. Travers came slowly towards him and she was big and stout and old, and she leaned on a stick as she walked. She had white hair and very bright blue eyes and she smiled with her eyes. Her voice was low and pleasantly modulated and like her smile very warm and friendly. Her mouth was the worst thing he had seen on a human face.

"I see, so you're from the Immigration Office and you want to ask me a few more questions about that poor lodger of mine. Thank you." She glanced at Michael's plain card and tucked it in her bag.

"Well, do come in, Mr. Howard. I hoped we'd finished with the wretched business when Inspector Ellis called yesterday, but if there is anything I can do to help you, I'm at your disposal." Once more came the warm smile from her eyes and the pleasant words from the gash of her mouth.

She wheeled on her stick and led him down the hall. She limped slightly, but unlike the maid, there were no puppet strings attached to her feet. Every step was firm and controlled; too firm. It was almost as if she spoke through her steps to the carpet, the floor boards and the joists that held them; right through to the earth below.

"I own you." They seemed to say. "Never forget that I own you. All of you, wood, cloth, leather and earth, you are mine and you belong completely to me."

As Michael watched those firm steps in front of him he sensed the thing that had made the mouth the shape it was.

She pushed open a door at the end of the passage and motioned him to follow her. The piano playing stopped as they came into the room. There was something rather unnatural about the way it stopped, as if the fingers were still pressing the keys but the wires were silent.

The two men in the room were different in age, size and appearance, yet they were alike. They were grey; everything about them was grey. They got up and looked at Michael and one was tall and old and the other was young and thick-set and neither of them mattered in the slightest. Only Mrs. Travers mattered.

Their faces were quite ordinary and commonplace and they both wore grey suits, but it was their expressions that gave them their greyness. Like the maid, they might have been shut out of the sun forever. As Michael looked at them and past them round the big, over-furnished room, he was suddenly reminded of the words before the Purgatorio. *"Abandon Hope All Ye Who Enter Here."*

"This is Mr. Howard from the Immigration Office in London. His department has sent him to make certain enquiries about the murder. It seems that the poor girl was a German." Mrs. Travers' voice broke on to his thoughts like cool water on fire.

"Mr. Howard, this is my son, Paul, and this is Mr. Rouse. Mr. Rouse might best be described as my U.P.G., my unpaying guest."

"How do you do." Michael took Rouse's hand and it felt cold

and dry and lifeless. It was like a germ of wheat that had died in its husk.

"Good afternoon, Mr. Howard. I do hope the police will get to the bottom of this murder soon. A terrible business, really terrible."

"Of course it is terrible, Frank, and of course everybody hopes that. Except, I suppose, the person who killed her." The woman smiled at Rouse and he drew back as if she had struck him. Michael was suddenly reminded of the keeper of a menagerie with her son, her maid and her unpaying guest; her shabby tigers.

"Yes, Mr. Howard. Mr. Rouse is a very great hoper. He lives in the hope that one day soon a long awaited legacy may materialize and he will be able to repay the back rent he owes me. It must be quite a respectable amount by now. Let me see, how long have you stayed with us, Frank? Yes, a long time isn't it? You arrived the month after my husband—died." Once more there came the slight pause between the words and Michael remembered Mrs. Carlton sitting in Hailstone's office. "Just after James was born, my husband—died."

"Please, please, Edith, not in front of strangers." Rouse's head bent lower and a dry tongue ran across his lips.

"And why not, Frank? Mr. Howard is a special kind of stranger; an investigator. He comes from a government department, and it is our bounden duty to tell him all our little secrets. Yes, yours as well, Paul." Her eyes flicked over to the boy by the piano.

"My son was very attracted to the murdered girl, Mr. Howard. He was also the last person to see her here. She left at four o'clock while I was out. I wonder if he killed her because she didn't respond to his advances." Crack went the whip and another animal drew back.

"No, that's foolish of me of course; he didn't kill her. He hasn't the strength to kill anybody. Besides he didn't go out of the house that night. He very rarely goes out. He prefers to sit at home and play the piano and imagine he is on the stage of a concert hall with a flock of young girls in jeans admiring him. He is very clever with the piano; he plays it with his feet."

Michael looked at him and there was a terrible pity in his eyes as he looked; pity and also wonder, for that boy could never have played at all. He was a cripple and his hands were tiny. They had withered at birth and there was nothing that could ever be done for him.

He glanced past him towards the piano and he saw why the playing had sounded so correct and dead. Above the keyboard there was an open panel that showed brass rollers and a ribbon of perforated paper, while below, the pedals were flat and much larger than normal practice. The thing was a pianola; a mechanical toy that played itself.

As he stood there, he suddenly had a dreadful desire to turn on his heel and walk quickly out of the room. Out into the air, away from Mrs. Travers and her menagerie, her dark house, her unpaying guest waiting for his legacy, her white-faced maid and her son sitting on the stool, dreaming of being a concert artist, while his feet pumped on the pedals to make the dead music.

Almost as if she had read his thoughts, the woman turned to him.

"No, Mr. Howard, I rather doubt if we can help you. In my opinion, the girl was just a type of girl who sooner or later would have got into trouble anyway, and most unfortunately she found the worst kind of trouble. She had very little to say for herself while she was here and we know nothing about her. In fact, she hardly spoke to anyone except Mr. Rouse and my son. Still, though I may not be able to help you, I can at least offer you a cup of tea." She walked past him and as her dress brushed against his coat, he noticed that it smelt slightly of camphor. Just as the door closed behind her, he heard her speak to the maid and her voice was quite different. It lost all traces of culture and modulation and became quite flat and toneless and without expression. "Grace," she said. "Tea."

"So sometimes the girl talked to you, Mr. Travers." Michael forced himself to smile at the son. "What did she talk about? Did she tell you anything about herself?"

"Oh, no, not about herself. She never said anything about herself. We just talked about music. She was very fond of music and she seemed to understand it. I liked her very much." His little hand ran across the lid of the piano and he didn't seem to be talking about a person at all, but just an idea. An idea of somebody who was young and fresh and liked music. A fresh presence in the dark house from which he rarely went out.

"Mr. Howard." Rouse took two steps toward him and there was a slight flush on his face. It was like something coming alive.

"Mr. Howard, I wonder if you would tell me something? When she died, that is, when she was killed—do you think that she would have suffered much?" The last words came out quickly, slurred and running together.

"Oh, yes, Mr. Rouse. I think she would have suffered. As far as the medical evidence can tell us she died quickly, but I think there would have been a great deal of terror. Yes, even under the drugs, she would have suffered." He watched the flush leave his face and fade. Then the door opened and Mrs. Travers came back into the room with the maid behind her.

"Put it down there." It wasn't a request or an order, just a statement, and like a piece of machinery set in motion by a switch, the woman lowered the tray on to the table and drew back. She was quite unlike anything that he had seen before. Not a help, or a servant or even a slave. As she looked at her mistress, he saw neither fear nor resentment in her eyes; only appeal. A stray dog pleading for a pat or a smile from that mouth which could never smile if it lived a thousand years.

"Well, Mr. Howard, are there any questions you would like to ask us?" His hostess poured out the tea and handed him a cup. "I am sure we will all try to be helpful."

And they were. As in every other visit they tried to be helpful. He asked the same questions as before and they told him nothing. The girl did not have any letters or callers. She did not seem to be frightened of anything. She talked very little, paid her rent and went out twice in the fortnight she was with them; the second time was to her death. As soon as he had finished his tea he pushed back his chair and stood up. From what these people knew, there seemed no reason for Gerda Raine to die and they could tell him nothing about her murder, only about human despair.

"Thank you, Mrs. Travers," he said, "you've all been most helpful."

"Not at all, it has been a pleasure. If any of us remembers anything we will contact the police." She stood up and held out her hand; once again he smelt the faint trace of camphor.

"Goodbye, Mr. Howard, Mr. Rouse will show you out."

Rouse walked very slowly to the door. His thoughts seemed to be a long way away. Just before Michael turned off the step he leaned forward towards him.

"Mr. Howard, please may I ask you another question? This boy the police arrested; yes, James Carlton. The policeman who came yesterday told me that he was in the clear and would be released. Is that really true?"

"Yes, that's quite true. He had witnesses to prove he had nothing to do with the actual murder and they let him go last night." Something in the man's eyes made him go on. "Tell me, Mr. Rouse, do you know the Carltons?"

"I know very few people these days, Mr. Howard. Once, perhaps, a long time ago—I . . ." He glanced quickly behind him and for a moment his left hand clutched Michael's arm. There was a lot of strength in his thin fingers.

"Mr. Howard, please listen to me. I don't know what your official position may be, but you've got to try and stop this thing. You see the police just don't realize what it really is, so you must let them know. Tell them—tell them that this isn't just a simple murder on its own but the beginning of something else."

There was a noise behind him and he broke off and slammed the door shut. Through the wood Michael could hear Mrs. Travers' limp coming towards him.

CHAPTER EIGHT

"And you're quite sure? The old boy didn't give you another word of explanation, just hooked it back to town?"

Michael sat staring at Penny in the lounge of the Three Mitres Hotel and his face was drawn and worried. The atmosphere around them was thick with pipe and cigar smoke as tired business men sprawled in the deep chairs and at the back of the enormous room of plush and mahogany, three aged ladies, piano, violin and cello, struggled their way through the "Maid of the Mountains."

"No, not a ruddy word. I just can't understand it. As soon as we left Mrs. Brett's house he seemed to close up. He muttered a few words to me which I didn't make head or tail of, and told me to tell the driver to take him to the station. When we got there, there was a train in, so he bought a ticket to London and went on it. That's the lot. Said something about our keeping out of mischief and he would ring you in the morning." She reached forward and laid her hand on Michael's knee.

"You know, Mike, I don't like it, I just don't like it. It's so odd and completely out of character. Have you ever known him behave like this before?"

"Never. Usually he's most forthcoming and tells me every move he intends to make. Everything in this damned case has been odd from the beginning." He lifted her hand and began to run his finger backwards and forwards across the palm. "Yes, my sweet, everything's quite odd and out of character. A murder that couldn't have happened unless you change the time theory, a man with crippled hands who plays the piano and, just to make things nice and easy, Kirk behaving in a way he's never done before." He looked past her at a commercial traveller who was turning the pages of his evening paper. For a second he caught a glimpse of a headline. "HUSBAND LEAVES MOTHER OF FIVE FOR ACTRESS."

"I wonder," he said, "I just wonder."

"What, Mike? What do you wonder about?"

"I'm not sure yet. About truth possibly. About respectable people who tell the truth as they see it, but for some reason it's not true. I wonder about that and something else. A link that somehow we've missed and which would make all these false truths come together." His fingers tightened round her hand and he looked very hard at her.

"Penny," he said. "I want you to try and think about the top of the stairs where Carlton said he left Gerda. Can you remember anything about it?"

"I suppose so, but what?" She frowned at him and thought for a moment. "It was very dark, with a lamp at the end of the road. There was the house with the lettering over the door and a little area at the top of the steps sunk into the wall. There was a rail leading down. It was very rusty and fixed by big spikes to the wall. Some of them were loose." She stopped suddenly and withdrew her hand. "Mike, stop it, you're hurting me."

"Sorry, darling, but I think I may have got it." He finished his drink and stood up. "I'm not sure yet but I want to try something. Look at it like this. We know that Gerda Raine was killed on the hour because of two things. The evidence of the tug skipper and the broken watch. I believe we've been wrong all the time. After all, people do dump things in rivers and run away, and that doesn't make them murderers. Suppose that it was that. At ten o'clock some quite innocent citizen was throwing garbage into the water and the man on the tug heard him. It all had nothing to do with the murder at all."

"But the watch, Mike. The watch and the two men who came up the steps and saw her. She was alive at six minutes to ten and the watch was stopped at ten. Please tell me what you're driving at, quickly."

"Just that she wasn't alive, darling and Carlton wasn't the fool we thought him, but a very bright boy. Stand up beside me and I'll show you how it was done. That's right, with your back to me. Now I want you to go quite limp and try and fall forward."

Quite oblivious to the curious stares from the other occupants of the lounge he gripped the belt of her dress and held her as she slid forward.

"All right, that does it, I think. You can relax now. Do you see what I'm after?"

"Yes, I see. It was the spikes wasn't it? The nails that held the rail; they held her too." Penny sat down and lit a cigarette. She dragged hard at it before she went on.

"Carlton killed her at the top of the stairs, didn't he? Just after he had killed her he must have heard the men coming up the stairs but he didn't panic. He hitched her body on to the nails and walked away in front of them as if nothing had happened. What they saw in the dim lamplight was not Gerda, but her dead body, hanging on the wall. The dog knew though, and he pulled back because he was frightened. Yes, the devil, the clever devil."

"Yes, as you say, very clever. He took the chance that nobody would turn up and find her and it worked. When he had gone with his witnesses and made sure they would recognize him he came back. He carried the body down the stairs and beat in the face with a piece of scrap iron. Then he set the watch back to ten and smashed it with the iron, making quite sure that a few splinters of glass had stuck to it. After that, all he had to do was to put her in the water and walk home with a guaranteed, twenty carat alibi. Fair enough, Penny?"

"Yes, fair enough. The bastard, the bright bastard. You're going to get him now, aren't you, Mike?"

"Yes, now I'm going to get him. I'm quite sure that was how he did it, but we'd never prove it in court. I'm going to see our friend Carlton now, and I'll get a confession from him if I have to beat him to pulp." He watched Penny's expression and shook his head.

"Oh, no, my dear, not this time. This I have to do alone. You stay here. Besides, the old man might change his mind and ring tonight and if he does, I want you to be here to tell him. Bye, darling, see you soon." For a second his hand brushed against hers, then he turned and walked out of the room. He felt suddenly very close to death.

The Carltons had a flat in one of the new council blocks on a bomb-site. They looked very tall and impressive among the small houses that clustered around them and were built of white brick which was just beginning to weather.

Michael parked the car that Hailstone had lent him, at the end of the main road and walked down a path which was lined with notices. They were all authoritative and of a forbidding nature.

"CYCLING FORBIDDEN," he read. "KEEP OFF THE GRASS,"

"DOGS MUST NOT BE ALLOWED TO FOUL THE FOOT-WAY," "DUST-BINS WILL BE READY FOR COLLECTION ON FRIDAY NOON."

The blocks themselves looked pleasant and cheerful with lights on the outside landings, but their names had a military and awe-inspiring ring. "Marlborough House," "Wellington House," "Kitchener," "Roberts," "Montgomery."

Michael pushed open the door of "Roberts" and walked to the lift. For the second time that day he smelt its medley of odor; new paint, new insulation, Jeyes Fluid, and faintly now, just beginning, unwashed humanity.

The Carltons lived on the top floor and it was the only flat there. The rest of the space was taken up with the water tanks and heating plant. There were red painted fire buckets at either side of the lift shaft. He walked past them to the door across the landing, raised the knocker and then went rigid.

There were voices coming through the wood of the door and he recognized them. The tones of one were quite normal and it belonged to Mrs. Carlton, but the other shouldn't have been there. It was high-pitched and hysterical and came from Rouse; the lodger with the awaited legacy who knew so few people.

Michael looked behind him and then bent his head against the door and listened. Rouse's voice was quite loud but his words were muddled and seemed to run together. "Must," he said. "Must stop—can't face it—carry on." And at each break there came a low reassuring murmur from the woman.

Michael listened for a moment then he peered through the key-hole and saw that the door opposite was closed. He reached in his pocket and pulled out a thin strip of spring steel. He bent it slightly and then worked it carefully into the gap between the door and the frame where the new wood had shrunk till it was pressing against the tongue of the lock. Then, with a quick pressure, he forced it home and the door opened. Less than a second later he saw his mistake.

"Mr. Howard!" The sitting-room of the flat was just across the hall and save for the flicker of a dying fire it was in darkness. It was the darkness that had made him think the door was closed. It was wide open and Rouse was standing in the doorway looking at him.

Michael straightened up from the lock and waited for the accusations, the tirade, the storm of reproach. They never came and Rouse was smiling. Like an impossible thing there was a smile on that worn, grey face and it looked completely friendly.

"Mr. Howard, you're here. You've come here just as I hoped you would. Believe me, it is like the answer to a prayer." He walked forward and laid his hand on Michael's arm. "Come in, my friend, please come in. There is so much that we have to tell you." He pulled him forward and he was like a child drawing a favorite uncle into a game.

Mrs. Carlton sat by the fire and she looked even smaller then before. Her feet rested on a cushion in front of her chair and they only just reached it. She was knitting; the needles clicked sharply together and they seemed red in the glow of the fire. She didn't even look up at Michael.

"Sally, you know Mr. Howard, don't you? He saw you this morning. I can't think why he has come back now, but I'm sure it's a sign to us; a sign that we must talk to him. Mr. Howard, before you start I must tell you something just in case you don't already know. James, poor James, is my son."

"No, I hadn't guessed that." He looked at Rouse and there was a resemblance in his face. Then he turned to the woman by the fire. And she reminded him of something too. It was her stillness, her silence and her compulsive knitting that reminded him. She was like a *tricoteuse* of the Revolution before the guillotine. "What are you knitting, Madame?" "Nothing of any importance, Monseigneur; only shrouds."

"No, Mr. Rouse, I didn't know that, but now I think I'm beginning to understand. You were the husband who—died. Why didn't you tell me this this afternoon?"

"I couldn't, Mr. Howard. You must believe that. I wanted to, I think I would have done if that woman hadn't come behind us. I just didn't dare, you see. I've never really dared anything very much in my life, I'm afraid, but now it's all gone too far. Far too far." He broke off and looked at the woman by the fire.

"Sally, don't you see? We must give up now and tell the truth. It may have started innocently, but now it's all gone too far and we've got to stop it before it happens again. You do see that, don't you, Sally?" His hands hung at his sides as he looked at her and there was a terrible pleading in his eyes, like a child begging his mother to postpone a visit to the dentist.

"Yes, before it happens again, Frank. That's what you're frightened of isn't it. What do you want me to say to Mr. Howard? How do you want me to tell him the truth; that we were once normal people who did something wrong? That we accepted something we didn't understand and now have to betray it. Oh no, my dear. Not now. There can be no betrayal now. We've gone too far and we will play this out, right to the last throw." She looked up at Michael and her voice was low and gentle and yet strong; very strong.

"Yes, Mr. Howard, I lied to you today. I told you my husband had died, but that wasn't true. He did something wrong and he left me, but he didn't die; at least not in the way you mean it. Later he met a dear friend of mine and that friend brought us together again. Now he wants to betray us."

She got up from her chair and stood in front of Rouse. Her head barely reached his shoulder but somehow she looked the taller of the two.

"No, Frank, there's been far too much betrayal in the past and you won't hurt any of us again. You're not going to injure the one thing I really care about. I'm so sorry, my dear, but I can't let you stop it." Her right hand came up to his forehead and slowly smoothed back a lock of grey hair. For a moment there was an expression of deep love in her eyes. Then it died. The hand reached down into her knitting and moved forward quickly. "Get the man, James," she screamed as the filed needle went for Rouse's throat.

The boy came from behind a curtain at the back of the room and his body was like iron. His hands took Michael's shoulders and his knee went home in the small of his back. There was no hold or muscle that could break the grip of those dreadful hands.

Michael didn't even struggle. He leaned back as the hands directed him and his own hands lay idly at his sides while his eyes watched the woman.

Her expression never altered. She stood quietly by the fire and looked at Rouse as he moved three times on the floor and then stopped moving. Then she bent down and took the needle. She wiped it and turned to Michael.

"That is a pity, Mr. Howard, a great pity. Please believe me when I tell you that I never wanted it to happen that way, but I have such a lot to protect." She smiled past him and Michael knew that she was smiling at the boy at his back with his hands clawing at his shoulders and his knee boring into his kidney. Even in his agony he could understand the love in her face and he dreaded what he might soon have to do.

"Yes, I have a lot to protect and possibly to die for. I'm very sorry but I'm afraid you will have to die as well, Mr. Howard. You will have to die without knowing the story and I think you will hate that more than anything." The needle was quite clean now. She laid down the wool and stepped over Rouse's body towards him.

"You want to know how and why the murder was done, don't you? Then ask me. Ask me any questions you like. Who was the old woman in the bar for instance, how was the time fixed, why did the girl have to die? Go on, my dear, ask me."

She said *my dear* and she meant it. Even as she came forward with the needle in her hand he knew that she meant it, because she hated what she had to do. To her he was just a boy in trouble and she was very sorry for him.

"Don't be frightened of me," she said, "because I won't hurt you. I promise that I won't hurt you. Please try and understand as well. You see, in this matter, I am just a servant." The needle moved upward and pressed below his Adam's Apple. "Now, ask your questions."

Michael looked into her eyes and suddenly he knew it was just a trick and she would tell him nothing. She was so gentle, so full of love and sympathy that she wanted to save him pain. She wanted him to start talking and forget death before she killed him. Just let him open his mouth and her needle would go home. It drew back a little and quivered in front of his eyes, waiting.

"Well, haven't you got anything to say to me?"

"Yes," he said. "Just one thing." And all at once he was tired of the Carltons and the Carlton secrets and the Carlton needles; sick and tired of them. Very gently he slid his hand downwards against the grip of the arms and felt it reach what he wanted.

"Catch," he said and the gun in his pocket exploded.

CHAPTER NINE

The train was late at Euston and the city had gone to bed; Kirk didn't care. As if he had all the time in the world he strolled across to the line of phone booths and dialled a number. It was listed as a private flat in Clapham but the bell was answered at the first ring and the voice of his secretary was on the line.

"Hullo, my dear," he said. "Sorry to ring you so late, but I want a little information and I regard you as my personal filing cabinet as you know. What's that you say? No, I'm not on holiday, far from it. Now listen; if I wanted to learn about certain obscure and primitive 'witch cults,' who would be the people to go to? I see, the Department of Ethnography at the Royal Albert Museum. Any idea of the curator's name? Ah, Thomas Baliol-Warde. He would be called something like that wouldn't he? As soon as the museum opens I want you to ring up this Mr. Warde and tell him I'll be round to see him about ten thirty in the morning. Got that? Right, goodnight then."

He replaced the phone and walked across the almost deserted booking-hall to the cab rank. He growled the address of his flat in the Cromwell Road to the driver and sank back against the cushions staring out at the darkened windows of Marylebone and Bayswater and he hardly saw them at all.

It could be, he thought. It could be like that, but on the other hand it might be something much simpler. The time had come to check both possibilities. He remembered the bulk of the "Rosa

Luxemburg" dark under the lights and he pulled back the partition and gave another address to his driver. He was going to see the one man who could tell him the truth; the man who would know, the horse's mouth, the man at the top.

The man lived in a big house off the Bayswater Road and the door had a flagpole over it and a brass plaque beside. Before Kirk had even taken his hand off the bell, the door swung open.

The butler looked quite ordinary and he was medium-sized, medium-colored and middle-aged. He wore a fawn jacket and striped trousers and his pocket bulged slightly as if he carried something heavy in it. He took Kirk's card and glanced at it but he didn't seem very interested.

"Will you wait here, please, while I make some inquiries." He shut the door, carefully, adjusted the chain and then walked across the thick red carpet to another door at the end of the hall. When he came back there was a big Alsatian bitch with him. It sat down on the floor and watched Kirk. It didn't seem to like the look of him very much.

The man patted the dog on the head and for a second a slight grin spread across his very ordinary face. "While I am seeing the doctor's secretary, Shura will look after you," he said, and walked up the stairs.

"Thank you, I am sure we will get on excellently together." Kirk looked at the big dog and smiled.

"Hullo, Shura," he said. "How are you? I wonder, my dear, I just wonder if that blighter in M.I.5. was right and they do train you people that way? Well, let's see for ourselves, shall we?"

Still talking very gently he walked towards the dog and held out his torn hand. Slowly its hackles rose, the muzzle wrinkled into a snarl while the rear muscles started bunching to spring. There was a rather sad and bewildered expression on its face. It didn't wish him any harm, but it knew its orders and its capabilities.

"Stand back," it seemed to be telling him. "Please stand back. I don't want to fight, but by jingo if I do."

"Take it easy," Kirk said. "Just take it easy, Shura, my lovely girl. Just let me get a little closer to you, my sweet. That's right, just another yard and we're there. Thank you, darling, we're close enough now."

He bent his head towards the snarling face and his voice changed to an urgent whisper. "Shura," he said, "Shura E vas lublu."

And the blighter from M.I.5. was right. As soon as she heard the words and the altered tone the dog's attitude changed. The snarl shrank to a foolish grin, the hind legs relaxed and the tail thumped heavily on the floor. Then she crept forward and rested her big head in Kirk's hand.

"What have you done? What do you want here?" The woman on the stairs was quite young and her mouth hung open as if she had just seen a ghost. It was a nice full mouth on a very pretty face.

Kirk turned and looked up at her. He looked at all of her and his eyes were alive with appreciation. Her face was lovely but lower down she was even better.

"I don't understand," she said. "That dog is supposed to be a killer. What have you done to her?"

"No secret, my dear. No poisoned meat, aniseed or any other parlor tricks. Just kindness and my own technique with all female creatures. Wonderful chaps with animals, we British; noted for it all over the globe. Now, may I see your master?"

"I don't know." She came down the stairs and stared at him. "Yes, you are Kirk aren't you? The man from British Intelligence. I remember seeing your photograph in the file. But what do you want here? Don't you realize where you are?"

"Yes, I realize where I am, and you are right about my name and my disagreeable occupation. Now do I see him?"

"Yes, yes, I suppose so. There is a form to be filled in of course." She moved to a desk and handed him a sheet of paper and a pen.

"Come off it, Comrade." Kirk replaced them on the desk and then lightly slapped her on her beautiful backside. It was a purely automatic action and it rather surprised him but the girl took it as a matter of course.

"Let me tell you something, my dear. If your master came to my office and was made to fill in a form, my secretary would soon wish she had never been born. Knowing the methods of your employers, I imagine you would look as if you never had been. Now, stop wasting my time and lift your little telephone and tell him that I'm here."

"Very well, at once. And thank you, sir." She picked up the telephone on the desk, waited for a moment and then spoke quickly and nervously into it. She was rewarded by a single gruff syllable in reply.

"Please come with me," she said and walked in front of him up the stairs. She was a very good person to walk behind.

The man at the top had a big room; everything about it was big. It was tall and wide and long and lit by fluorescent tubes with furniture that might have come from an exhibition of bad Victoriana. There were glossy oil-paintings on the walls and a gilt mirror stood at the back. There was a desk in front of the mirror and behind the desk there was a little fat man eating an apple. He put it down as Kirk came in and smiled at him. He was a great little smiler and he looked friendly and respectful as he stood up in his dark suit with the light shining on his bald head. He could have been the manager of a branch bank, rising to greet Mr. Onassis. He wasn't a banker. His name was Peter Kun, and, as the saying goes, he had killed more than the cholera.

"Welcome, my dear confrère, welcome to my castle. Or should I say my parlor?" He laughed hugely, and his three little chins shook over his collar. His laugh was quite false and without meaning. It was just part of the elaborate façade that hid his real self and even included his official position. He was listed as third legation secretary, but in reality, he was head of all Soviet espionage groups in Western Europe and answerable only to Colonel-General Serov in person.

He took Kirk's hand and beamed at him. "You know, you are a brave fellow to come here. I wonder what I should do with you. Perhaps I should try to smuggle you to Russia, disguised as a crate of confidential papers. I wonder if I could get away with it. They might give me an Order of Lenin for you. No, I suppose not." He shook his head sadly. "Knowing your reputation I'm quite sure you will have such a scheme all wrapped up." He came nearer to Kirk and patted his arm. Kirk noticed that he smelled slightly of scent.

"I hear that you've been a bad chap downstairs and already corrupted a loyal member of my staff. Tell me, how did you steal the affections of the dog?"

"Very simple, Dr. Kun. I have read the works of your Professor Pavlov with his conditioned reflexes and somebody told me that you train your guard-dogs like that with a system of passwords. He also said he thought he knew the phrase used in this building. I wanted to see if he was right."

"And he was right, he was quite right. 'Shura E vas lublu.' Shura, I love you." Kun laughed again and little beads of sweat shone on his forehead.

"Oh, dear, you'll be the death of me, General, you really will. Wonderful chaps with animals, you British, quite wonderful. However, we have our tricks too, where human beings are concerned; Spencer, for example." He mentioned the name of a physicist who had recently fled to the East.

"Now tell me something, my friend; something which is important and which I would very much like to know." He laid his hand on Kirk's shoulder and lowered his voice.

"When you were downstairs with Sonia, my secretary. Did you do something to her? Did you perhaps slap her bottom? You did. Excellent." His hand thumped Kirk's shoulder and he led him to a chair.

"In that case I think we will get on. It's an odd thing but everybody who ever comes here has to slap poor Sonia's bottom. From office boy to British General they do it. Even Mr. Khrushchev himself has slapped Sonia's wonderful bottom.

"Poor Sonia and poor Shura. What must I do with Shura now that you know her one trick? Perhaps they will take her home and put her in a Sputnik to annoy your old women in Cheltenham."

He crossed to a cupboard and took out a long, clear bottle. The cupboard itself was heavily carved with mahogany nymphs and vine-leaves. Generations ago, Kirk could have imagined a grand old English gentleman with side-whiskers reaching into it for the port. Just above it there was a large oil painting of Voroshilov. The canvas was new and glossy but the frame was old. Not long ago it had probably housed a picture of Bulganin. He wondered how long Voroshilov would be allowed to occupy it.

"Well, here we are." Kun placed two glasses on the desk and raised his own. "As you say, Cheerio." He drained his vodka in a quick practiced movement and laid it down.

"Now, General Kirk, to business." Like a light going out, his face changed and all humor and goodwill left it. As Kirk looked at that cold face he knew that everything he had heard about Dr. Kun would be the exact truth.

"Just what do you want from us?"

Kirk didn't answer him at once. He drank his vodka slowly and he thought before he spoke. If he was going to get what he wanted he had to play his cards just right.

"No, Doctor," he said. "That's the wrong start; not us, just you. I want to ask you a purely personal favor and it has nothing to do with our politics or our—professions. I will give you my word for that."

"A personal favor from—me." Kun's forehead wrinkled slightly and he played with the empty glass on the table. "You know, it is a very long time since anybody used the word personal in my presence. Very well, General, I will accept your word and change my question. What do you want from *me?*"

"Just the answer to something. If I get it I will be able to know the end of a story which started while you were in charge of the Berlin department two years ago."

"Yes, I was in Berlin. What about it, my friend?" There was very little interest in his eyes.

"While you were there, I think you had working for you a German girl whose name was Gerda Raine?"

"Ahah. Yes, here it comes. You are quite right, Gerda Raine was on my pay-roll. Poor little Gerda who has recently met such a terrible end."

"You know that!" Kirk leaned forward and stared at him. "How do you know, Dr. Kun?"

"For the time being, let's say that I have friends; lots of friends and sometimes they tell me things. I know all about her you see, and I have kept, shall we say, a fatherly eye on her from time to time since she reached this country. She was called Gladys Reeves, wasn't she?" He reached out for the bottle and refilled the glasses.

"Tell me, General. You don't really believe we killed her, do you?"

"No, you didn't kill her. At first I thought you might have, since you had an excellent reason for wishing her dead, but it wouldn't have been that way. No, I fancy I know your methods by now, Dr. Kun." He lifted his glass and smiled at him.

And Kun smiled too. His face broke into little creases and his eyes came alive. He reached out to the intercom and spoke a few sentences in Russian.

"So, you know our methods, do you? I wonder if you knew Gerda's. Let me tell you something. As I said, I followed her with a fatherly interest. Until a little over a month ago, she was living in London. Then a man turned up. We never knew his name, but she went away with him. We couldn't trace her till we heard she was dead. Thank you, Sonia."

He watched his secretary come into the room and lay a packet on the desk. There was a slightly proprietary expression in his face as he looked at her. She bowed to Kirk and went out.

"Now, my friend, I am going to show you something which will prove I speak the truth. We didn't kill Gerda and we had no reason to wish her dead. On the contrary we owed her a deep debt of gratitude. I think this should help you to understand what I mean." He opened the package and pushed the contents across to him. It was the photostat of a page of typescript.

"You see, Gerda had nothing to fear from us. It was you she cheated all the time. When she took the papers from the stupid Captain Richmond, she made a picture of them with a little Leica camera I had given her. Then she rang your people and mine. She sold you the original for five hundred pounds and a passport, and we got the copy. We were quite satisfied with it."

"I see. Check to you, Dr. Kun, and my congratulations." Kirk pushed the film back to him without bothering to read it. He had utter faith in his statements. "May I ask you what her price to you was?"

"Of course you may. It was just my word. The word of a little, quite untrustworthy Hungarian Jew who had betrayed his country, his family and his friends in the service of a foreign power. She wanted my promise that when she went over I would leave her alone. Strangely enough, I did. I watched her movements but I left her in peace. I wonder why I did that? Perhaps I had an affection for her." He flicked the film with his forefinger and it rolled across the desk to Kirk.

"Keep that as a souvenir, my friend. It is of no further use to me. I understand that the sites were changed at the last NATO meeting.

"Gerda was a bright girl, wasn't she? She got the best of both worlds; a country from you and freedom from me."

"Yes, she was bright, very bright." Kirk echoed his words automatically and he knew they were wrong. Only at the beginning had she been bright. She had got what she was after from both of them and as a guarantee of her safety she had accepted the word of the man at the top. The one man who would keep it. The old fox who had deceived so many of the great that he would honor his promise to one little, unimportant girl.

And after that what had this bright girl done? Had she benefited from her actions, made money or married well? She had done none of these things. For all her brightness the best she could get was a menial job, a tiny bedroom with a carved figure on the wall and at last the death of a drab.

"She was very attractive, you know, General Kirk. That might have been it." Kun frowned slightly as if he himself were puzzled that he had kept his promise. "I like to have attractive women in my office.

"Now, what do you want to ask me?"

"Just what she was really like, Doctor. Who was the real person called Gerda Raine. I know nothing, you see. I know she was a bright girl who got the better of both of us, I know she was a virgin, I know she was killed in a horrible way. And that is almost all I know—" He broke off and stared across the desk.

"What was that you said?" The Hungarian stood up and something started to happen to his face. He knocked over his glass and a stream of vodka poured across the desk. "What nonsense are you telling me?"

"That she was killed horribly." For a moment Kirk thought the man had gone mad. He got up and stood swaying in front of him with his hands clutching his side and tears running down his fat cheeks. His whole body shook and he was laughing. When at last he managed to speak he choked over the words.

"No, not that. What you said before." He pulled a handkerchief from his pocket and wiped his eyes.

"General Kirk, you are a naughty man. You come here into my territory and you do bad things. You make a fool of my dog and I don't mind. You slap my secretary on the backside and I still don't mind. I am very nice to you. I talk to you and I give you a drink; two drinks. Then what do you do to me, you terrible fellow? You insult me. You insult me deeply."

He pushed back his handkerchief and sank into the chair. "You know me and you must know my reputation. You know that Gerda worked for me and I have told you I was fond of her; yet you come here and tell that damned lie about her."

"Then you mean—"

"I mean that you are wrong and you insult me and it seems our little friend has fooled you again. You've got the wrong girl, General. It couldn't have been Gerda Raine you found in the river because she was not a virgin; I, Peter Kun, give you my word that she was not a virgin."

CHAPTER TEN

Mrs. Mott, Kirk's confidential secretary, sat as far back from the desk as she could with a short-hand pad on her knees. She had mild grey eyes behind glasses, hair done up in a bun and a jersey that was starting to unravel at the neck. She looked quite unlike Sonia Vronsky and just at the moment she was suffering from the heat.

Although it was August and London was scorching, the General kept his office windows tightly closed and an electric fire glowed in front of the desk. The heat and the cigar smoke made the atmosphere like an Eskimo's nightmare of the tropics. Kirk leaned far back in his chair staring at the ceiling as he listened to Michael's voice on the intercom. The phone was connected to its speaker but there was a loose wire somewhere and his words had an oddly distorted and nasal quality.

"No, son," he said quietly when Michael had finished his report. "No, I'm afraid that I can't compliment you on the way things have gone but there is no need to reproach yourself unduly. You're quite sure that you really did kill her, I suppose."

"Yes, sir, quite sure. I shot to kill. I had to. The needle was just about home and I knew I couldn't break Carlton's grip. I had to kill her, sir." Even through the faulty speaker, Kirk could detect the traces of hysteria in his voice.

"That's all right, Mike. I'm not blaming you, so just take it easy. A filed knitting needle can be a very nasty little weapon, especially when somebody is holding your arms.

"Now, let's get this right. You killed the woman and her son promptly knocked you out? You were unconscious for about twenty minutes and when you came round they had both disappeared and so far Captain Gallstone and his lads in blue have been unable to trace them?"

As he listened to Michael he could picture the first part of the act; the woman reeling backwards under the thirty-three to fall beside Rouse and the son reaching for the paper-weight and clubbing Michael. And then, what? Had he lifted his mother's body and carried her out alone or had somebody else come to help him? Somebody who understood a great deal about the concealment of bodies.

"Now, listen to me, son," he said. "Whatever you and the police may think, the murder was not done like that. No, I've no proof, but I'm quite sure about it and the reality was much worse and a great deal more subtle than what you imagine. The Carltons do not really matter at all. Remember her words; 'I am just a servant.' It is up to us to find her master.

"The Carltons may have helped to kill the girl and Rouse knew about it but they were not the prime-movers and don't really matter. That woman didn't kill Rouse to save her son, but for quite a different reason. I think I've almost found that reason and later today I'm coming back to Minechester and I'm going to introduce you to the man at the top; the person who is able to organize a quite impossible murder with so many reliable witnesses."

He ground out his cigar into the ash-tray and looked at a rough sketch on the desk. He had taken a lot of trouble with it and it showed a native carving with broken and reversed joints.

"No, Mike, I'm sorry but your way is wrong. It was quite a good theory, but it didn't happen like that. As I told you the body they found was not Gerda Raine, but somebody who looked like her and wore her ring; the ring that Captain Hugh Richmond gave her. I think we should pay a little more attention to Richmond, you know. He may have a niche in the story. He was nobody himself, but he might have had friends who remembered him. Yes, what is it Kipling says? 'It may be the bear is his mother.' I wonder?

"Now, this is what we are going to do. At exactly eleven o'clock tonight, if all goes well, I intend to call on this person who is able to arrange such convenient murders. Oh, no, we won't be able to arrest him; he's not that kind of person at all. All we can hope to do is to stop him for a time. That is, of course, if we're lucky and you and Penny put in a bit of work for me. I want Penny to go visiting and you Mike, are going to interest yourself in theology. Yes, that's right, theology; the science that treats of God and man's duty towards him.

"In a minute Mrs. Mott will give you your instructions, but first I think it fair to give you a rough resumé of what I learned since I called on our friend Dr. Kun." He gave a slight grin towards the intercom. "Dr. Kun, who, if his boasts are true, makes Casanova sound restrained. Now, if we're going to break this thing, it's imperative that you understand exactly what we're up against, so listen carefully. Good, well, as soon as the damned place opened, I paid a visit to the Royal Albert Museum—"

The Royal Albert Museum stood at the back of a Bloomsbury square and it looked rather like St. Pancras Station. It had a tower, pinnacles and even a gargoyle or two but didn't run to a lift. It seemed about a mile high and Mr. Baliol-Warde lived on the top floor.

Kirk marched endlessly down passages and up marble stairs, flanked by Roman busts, stuffed apes, sedan chairs and note-taking German students in leather shorts. On the third landing he found his way blocked by a large party of school children in charge of a pretty girl with a serious expression.

"Please, Miss Howland." A bullet-headed youth with a jersey and a studious expression stared at a pile of bones in a case. They were labelled "Bantu male. Indigenous African Native." "Why is it that all the African ones have bow legs?"

Kirk paused and waited for her answer. He was glad of a rest and had strong theories of his own on the subject of Bantu legs. She didn't even bother to reply, but waved "bullet-head" to one side and turned to a small girl who was interested in the structure of the thighs.

Feeling this was less than fair, Kirk leaned forward and tapped "bullet-head" on the shoulder.

"Good question, my boy. Shows you've been using your eyes, which is pretty rare these days. The answer is quite simple; no real mystery about it at all. The fact is that the chaps haven't been walking on 'em for long." He smiled at the teacher's look of fury and disgust, lifted his hat and moved on towards his goal.

"Ah, good morning, sir." Mr. Baliol-Warde stretched out a limp hand, permitted Kirk to shake it and waved him to a stiff-backed chair that was piled high with books and papers. "Do sit down," he said. "Push all that rubbish on the floor." He was tall, stooping and almost completely hairless.

"Now, let me see, Mister—er—yes, Kirk." He took the card, squinted at it and dropped it into an empty tray marked "out."

"Yes, of course, General—er—Kirk, from the Foreign Office, isn't it? You wanted to see me about something or other, was that it? You know I have an idea that I recently received some communication regarding you."

"You would have done, Mr. Baliol-Warde, less than half an hour ago. My secretary was told to phone you and she doesn't make mistakes." Kirk's eyes flickered past him round the room. It was filled with weapons, pieces of broken pottery and lengths of bamboo; there was an old-fashioned typewriter on the littered desk and somebody had laid a Polynesian devil-mask beside it. It looked like a piece of still-life done by a maniac and might have had a caption beside it. "This patient was admitted on such and such a date suffering from—"

"Yes, now you mention it, I believe she did. I seem to remember your name. As a matter of fact I think I made a note of it, but things get so out of place here. Now, where can it be?" He rummaged among the papers on his desk and then gave it up.

"No, I'm afraid it seems to have gone. We're always so pressed for work up here that at times we tend to forget the old maxim. 'A place for everything, and everything in its place,' eh, Mister—sorry, General Kirk?" As he uttered the title, a faint gleam of hope spread across his face.

"I say, I suppose it was this department you wanted, General; not Colonel Proctor in the military section by any chance?"

"No, not Colonel Proctor, Mr. Warde; I'm afraid you're the man I'm after. That is if you are the ethnographical expert of course."

"Oh, dear, the expert. That's a word I so much dislike. Still, I suppose it is my subject, and if there is any way I can help or advise you, I am at your service." He took off his glasses and polished them with a piece of blotting paper.

"That's most kind of you and I'll try to take up very little of your valuable time. I merely want you to identify something for me if you can." Kirk took the drawing from his pocket and handed it to Baliol-Warde.

"This is the rough sketch of a carving I saw recently. It is probably very badly done and was just intended to give the rough idea. I would like to assure you that I am not asking you this out of idle curiosity and it may be important. I seem to remember hearing something about carvings like that and they had some kind of significance and meaning. If you can help me to discover that meaning I will be deeply indebted to you."

"Very nice of you to say so. Let's have a look anyway." Warde pushed the typewriter to one side and laid the paper flat on the table, then he switched on a green shaded lamp and bent over it; he looked at the head first.

"Yes, jolly little fellow, isn't he? Blind, too. Very bad copy of course, look at the carving of the head. Obviously been done by somebody who has no idea of the process involved." He shook his head sadly and picked up a pencil. A mass of papers fell to the floor as his arm touched them but he didn't seem to notice it.

"Now, let's see where you come from." The pencil ran over the lines of the head exaggerating the details. "Yes, there's a lot of Negro influence of course, but there always is in this kind of thing. You can see it in the way they've dealt with the grain. There are other things though; Indian and Chinese certainly, and possibly North African as well. Yes, and something else which I don't understand, but it might be European. Where did you see this, General, and what do you want to know about it?"

"I saw it yesterday in a town in the North. It seemed important at the time; so important that I came to town specially to ask you about it. Mr. Warde, what do you know about this, what does it signify, who are the people who made it?"

Baliol-Warde didn't seem to hear him. He peered keenly at the pencilled lines and for the first time he looked slightly interested.

"Ahah, got you. Yes, it's quite clear now. This thing is Oceanic. That is the term we use for the East African islands; Madagascar, Mauritius, the Seychelles. The races and basic cultures there are so mixed up that at times it's difficult to spot the true origin. I can't help you much more, I'm afraid, as it's not my province really. The chap you want is Mr. Sykes but he's out of England at the moment. Perhaps if you were to come back in a month—Just a minute though."

His eyes moved from the face to the body and his expression changed. For a moment this muddled, bored and preoccupied man looked excited and efficient. He ran his pencil over the reversed joints and then he got up and rummaged in a filing cabinet in the corner. Here at least his system seemed to work; almost at once he found what he was looking for and handed it to Kirk. It was a similar drawing but done with much greater skill and attention to detail and it showed the same figure.

"Yes, that's your boy. No doubt about it at all. And you say that you found it in England. Now tell me something, General Kirk. From what you have told me, I gather that your interest is of a serious nature. Just how serious? Has it to do with death for instance; the death of a young woman perhaps?"

"Yes, you're quite right on both counts, Mr. Warde." Kirk stared at him as if he had worked a miracle. "Well, what is it? Is this thing some kind of fetish or fertility symbol?"

"Oh, no, nothing like that. This is something that is supposed to have died a long time ago; it should have died. Its origins are purely European and it has nothing to do with a fetish which is a sign of protection or a fertility symbol. This, General, is a talisman of decay." He rummaged in a drawer, found a notebook and scribbled something out of it on a scrap of paper.

"Just now I asked you if this carving you saw had been connected with a specific form of violence and you told me it had. I don't think I should try and tell you any more as I am not an expert and it might be wrong in some details. If I was, it might lead to complications. Here is the address of somebody who will be able to tell you about it. Go and see that person, go at once." He folded the paper and handed it to Kirk.

"You see, this creature is the symbol of a Satanic cult that is supposed to have died years ago. From what you say, it seems that it may not have died. If that is the case, I can envisage some very nasty possibilities. The name of the cult was originally 'Albert le Petit.'"

"'Albert le Petit.' 'Little Albert.'" Kirk's mind raced backward and he was standing at the top of the steps to the river, looking at the decayed building with lettering over the door. *'Alberti Minimi Sacris Laus et Gloria Magistri.'*

"'Little Albert,' it doesn't sound very sinister, Mr. Warde."

"No, it doesn't, does it? Rather comical in fact. It's not comical, though." Warde's long, sheepish face looked quite different. "Go to my friend, General. Ask the same questions you have asked me and then, if you can, put a stop to this business. Stop it quickly, because I promise you that there is nothing at all comic about 'Petit Albert.'"

CHAPTER ELEVEN

Warde's contact, Dr. Malan, shared part of a big house at the top end of Wimpole Street. It had an imposing line of brass plaques beside the door but could have done with a coat of paint.

Kirk studied the names and found what he was looking for at the end of the list; a very shiny and new strip of metal inscribed, "Dr. G.W. Beresford-Malan M.D. M.R.C.S. General Consultant and Practitioner in Psychological Therapy." He pressed the bell above it, stood on the step for a good two minutes and was at last admitted by a harassed man-servant who obviously did duty for all the tenants. He handed him his personal card, apologized for calling without an appointment and settled himself down in a big gloomy room, prepared for a long wait. There was a copy of "Hound and Heather" on the table. He picked it up as a time-killer and idly turned the pages.

He wasn't disappointed. On the very first page after the advertisement for dogs, whips and sporting guns there was an article in heavy type. It carried the heading "Plain Murder" and was an outspoken and scabrous attack on Western Chemical Industries and their plant on the River Taff. At the foot of the page he saw that its origin and authorship were proudly proclaimed. "Nantwood Hall—Nantwood—Northumberland," he read. "From Fetherstone Clumber-Holt Esq."

"Mr. Kirk, will you please come with me? I very much dislike seeing patients without an appointment, but I am prepared to fit you in for a short time. This way."

Dr. Malan was quite young, quite nice looking and dressed from head to foot in white. It made a dramatic contrast, for she was a full-blooded Negress.

She led Kirk out of the room and across the hall to a little surgery at the back of the house. It seemed to have sparse equipment, though he saw a cot, a desk, a case packed with bottles and a wash-basin; there was a very stout Negro bending over the basin with syringe in his hands. Kirk opened his mouth to explain the purpose of his visit, but was at once cut short.

"Oh, no, no, Mr. Kirk, we do not start like that. I have no desire to hear what you *think* is wrong with you, I much prefer to see for myself. Just stand still." She switched on a big lamp and tilted it at his face. As the beam hit him, he suddenly felt that he had become a character out of "Uncle Tom's Cabin" and the racial aspect of slavery had been most unfortunately reversed.

"Yes, yes, I see. It's all very clear." The woman put her hands on her hips and looked him up and down. Her wide lips made an odd clucking sound.

"Yes, there's no need to tell me anything at the moment, I can see it for myself. Yes, you've lived well, haven't you; too well. You take no exercise to speak of and keep out of the fresh air. Neurosis, too, I can see it plainly in your face. You probably suffer from unpleasant dreams. Physically, I should say that you eat too much, drink too much and your lungs will be coated with nicotine. Your blood pressure is certainly high and you could do with at least a stone of flesh off you." Her fingers suddenly shot out and dug him hard and painfully in the stomach.

"Still, we won't worry about the body for a moment. It's your mental state that worries me and I can see a most unpleasant expression on your face. Very well, let's get on with it. Just lie down on the couch will you? No, no, Mr. Kirk, I want no argument. Mr. Morgan-Phillips, will you please help the patient off with his clothes?"

The big negro put down the syringe he was washing and came up behind Kirk. He put his hands on his jacket and began to pull. It was not so much the gesture of helping anyone off with their clothes, as tearing them to pieces by the seams. As he felt the fingers behind him, rage completely blacked out Kirk's conscious mind and he became a pure and furious automaton. He leaned forward, clutched at the thick neck and gave a sudden jerk. The next moment, Mr. Morgan-Phillips flew over his shoulder and landed heavily on his back in front of Dr. Malan.

She took it quite calmly, in fact she seemed pleased, as if her diagnosis had been splendidly confirmed.

"Yes, just as I thought, homicidal tendencies as well. Very well, Mr. Phillips, you may go, and I will deal with this poor fellow myself." She watched her assistant limp slowly out of the room and then beamed at Kirk.

"Now, that's all right isn't it? We are quite alone and you have nothing more to be afraid of. Just do as I say, lie down on the couch so that I can examine you."

"Madam." Kirk struggled for control of breath and temper and counted five slowly. His face had a dark purple flush and he looked not so much like a sufferer from blood pressure as someone in the last stages of the Black Death. "Dr. Malan, I am afraid you are the victim of a misunderstanding. I have not come here for medical treatment or to consult you professionally, but on a purely personal matter which your friend Mr. Baliol-Warde said—"

"What! What is that you say?" If her face could have darkened it would have done. "You have not come here to consult me professionally but on a personal matter! What can Mr. Warde have been thinking of to send you round here during surgery hours? And you, sir, I would remind you that my time is valuable if yours is not. Why, I am a graduate of both Foulah Bay and Watford universities and not accustomed to—"

"Please, Dr. Malan, please listen to me for a moment. I am sorry I lost my temper and manhandled your assistant, but this matter really is important. I would never have ventured to take up your valuable time if Mr. Warde had not assured me that you were the only person who could help."

"I see. The only person who could help." She still frowned, but there was a happier expression on her face. "Very well, what is it you want from me?"

"I want to know what this is, Doctor." Kirk reached in his pocket and handed her the drawing. "Mr. Warde told me it was the symbol of a cult that once existed off the East African coast. I wonder if you can tell me any more?"

"Let me see it." She took it from him and held it under the light. Almost at once her face changed. The frown and all expression went out like a lamp switched off and her eyes grew wide and staring. She swayed for a moment and leaned against the desk.

"L'Albert," she said slowly. "Le petit Albert. Where did you get this, Mr. Kirk? This thing is death. It is 'Maksur Walad'—'The Broken Child'—'The Very Holy Thing'!"

Kirk watched her before replying and as he looked, he knew that to her the thing she was holding was fear. It was fear with two faces like a playing card and they were both watching her. It was the Negro witch-doctor and the white devil; all they had done, the forest rites, the drums, the slave ships and the tortures were looking at her from that rough scrap of paper.

"I found the original of this in the room of a friend of mine who died. I may be wrong but I have a feeling, just a feeling that this image might have had something to do with the death of my friend."

She nodded, but she didn't answer him at once. She crossed to the basin and filled a glass of water, then she took a bottle of small green tablets from the shelf, swallowed one and drank. When she turned, he saw that the fear had gone from her eyes and she was once more quite normal and very European and civilized.

"I am sorry, Mr. Kirk. I shouldn't have spoken like that, but seeing that picture upset me. It is nothing really, just a primitive superstition that was once brought to my people from yours."

"From my people, Doctor. Then this thing is European?"

"Oh, yes, it's origin is purely European. It started during your Dark Ages"—there was a slight accentuation of the adjective—"as a simple cult of the Devil. There were two forms which were known as 'Albert le Grand' and 'Albert le Petit.' It is the second one that concerns us. It is all well documented and you can read about it in Montague Summers." She broke off for a moment and lit a cigarette. She inhaled deeply and sat down on the edge of the cot.

"At the beginning this cult was identical to a hundred others. It was the usual kind of thing; a looking-back to the old gods, Pan, Hecate, Set-Osiris and merging them as an anti-Christian symbol. There was nothing important about it and it should have died."

"But it didn't die, did it, Doctor?" Under her manner, Kirk could still see a little of the frightened child looking out at him.

"But it didn't die, it survived. It hung on in one small area in France till the Revolution began. Then it changed its form and it began to grow.

"You will remember that during the 'Terror' many Frenchmen fled abroad. Some of them came here, some went to other parts of Europe and a great number went even farther afield to the French colonies, including Mauritius. On at least one emigree ship Petit Albert went too and I'm afraid that among my people he found very fruitful ground."

"You mean that it became some kind of Voodoo cult?" As he listened to her, Kirk's theory began to weaken. This was not what he had expected or wanted to hear. Nothing like this had killed a girl disguised as Gerda Raine. No woolly heads bowing before the fire as they offered cocks to Papa-Loy had taken her to the river. He was on the point of believing that he was wrong from the start when she went on.

"Yes, in one form you might call it that, I suppose. In Mauritius and the Seychelles it was similar to Voodooism; just childish nonsense and a source of annoyance and embarrassment to the missionaries. Nothing more. When it reached Madagascar however, it was to become quite different.

"Tell me, Mr. Kirk. Have you ever heard of a person called Ranavalo the Cruel?"

"Ranavalo? Let me think." Kirk frowned and for a moment his hand drummed quietly on the wall behind him.

"Yes, I think so. She was one of the queens of Madagascar wasn't she? About the middle of the last century."

"She was *the* queen, the great queen; the greatest of a line of female rulers and she held Madagascar for over thirty years. During those years it is possible that she killed more than Attila and Tamerlaine put together." As she spoke, Kirk knew that to the educated, westernized Dr. Malan, Ranavalo was not just a name from history but a thing of terror.

"If you are to understand what I am trying to tell you, Mr. Kirk, you must try and picture this woman. She was educated, yet she worshipped idols. She was always dressed in the height of Paris fashion, yet she lived in seclusion; too holy to be approached by her people. She relied on European advisors, but she ruled by threat of torture and her avowed aim was the destruction of all manhood except in the Hova tribe. At the same time, this woman was a doting and loving mother to her only son."

"I see," Kirk's hand stopped drumming on the wall and he stood quite still, staring at her. Like pieces of a puzzle the facts were fitting together. The queen who worshipped idols, the brightly dressed woman who lived alone, the destroyer of all virility and the good mother.

"Go on, Doctor," he said. "What was the connection between Ranavalo and 'Petit Albert'?"

"There was a man called Jean Laborde. He was an engineer and he was shipwrecked on the Madagascar coast. He became the slave of the queen and later the greatest man on the island. He built her arsenals and foundries for guns. Through him she was able to equip an army capable of driving back a combined force of French and English. I think that he may have done something else to her. It was about the time of Laborde's arrival that she first heard of Petit Albert."

"I see, and she changed it to her own ends?"

"Oh, yes, she changed it. It ceased to be a popular devil cult and took on a more private role reserved to the queen and her intimates. She put away her own idols; snakes and precious stones and became herself a deity. The all-powerful mother figure, with this her symbol." She took the paper from the desk and handed it back to him.

"Thank you." Kirk took the paper and glanced at it. Everything was clear now. This was the broken boy, the man who could never escape because its limbs hinged backward, the talisman of decay.

"And I suppose the son became part of the cult?"

"Oh, yes, he was part of the symbol. He had once been a Christian, it seems, but because she loved him, she left him in peace. Once the new religion had started however, she changed. He pleaded for the lives of certain prisoners who were to be killed and she put him away. She loved him very much and he was kindly treated on the whole. He was put away in a nicely furnished room below the ground and left there. From time to time they lowered food and water to him. I understand that he lived to be quite an old man."

"Thank you, Doctor, thank you very much indeed." Kirk smiled at her for he was almost home. In his own mind there was no doubt left. It could have been that way and if it was there was no problem as to why Gerda Raine's substitute had died.

A cult of women, he thought. Strong women with weak sons, whom they dominate; women whose husbands have left them perhaps for someone younger and fresher; women with one thought left, the protection of the sons who they dread may leave them. As he thought of this, he could almost see the faces of Mrs. Carlton, Mrs. Brett and Mrs. Travers looking at him and he heard their words. "My husband—died." "He was a medical missionary and he travelled a great deal. He did nothing remarkable, he just—died." "You came here, Mr. Rouse, just after my husband—died."

But the husbands had not died, they had gone away. Mr. Carlton hadn't died; he had changed his name to Rouse and after his fling had become the lodger of the formidable Mrs. Travers. And if she had been a friend of his wife the circle was complete.

Just given the possibility of that and he had the truth. Given a number of women like that and everything was clear; always supposing that they heard the story of Ranavalo the Cruel. And why couldn't they have heard it? One woman he had seen had been the wife of a medical missionary and in her house had been the carving. Suppose that she had come back after her husband's end with the knowledge and also the bitterness. Suppose that, quite by chance, that woman had seen the house with the carved inscription on the lintel and revived the cult in England. And then what? What would have made it once more a killer?

Perhaps a little go-getting girl like Gerda Raine who had threatened to take away one of those weak, well-loved sons. He needed just one more piece of information to make suspicion a certainty.

"Thank you, Doctor. Just two more questions and I will leave you in peace. Did this cult continue after the death of Ranavalo or did it end with her? If it has survived, do you imagine it ever spread to Europeans?"

"I don't know," she said and her voice was far away and distant. "It carried on for a time under the three queens that followed her, but in a milder form. Since then—who knows? Remember, it started in medieval France and crossed half the world before Jean Laborde took it to Madagascar. Now it is just a folk tale to frighten children, but who can tell. To me it seems unlikely that anything so tenacious of life would die easily.

"Now, Mr. Kirk, I have told you what I know about this business, so tell me something. Just what is your interest in Petit Albert?"

"Sorry, Doctor. I'm most grateful for your help, but I can't tell you at the moment. My hands are tied. One day, perhaps, I will be free to tell you and if so I will come back and let you know. Till then, goodbye, and thank you." He smiled at her, bowed and walked out of the door.

When he had gone, the woman stood quite still, staring in front of her. Then she reached for the telephone.

She was a long time in getting connected because the "Royal Albert" did not run to an efficient switch board. When at last she did, Baliol-Warde's voice was at the end of the line.

"Tom," she said, "that man you sent me. Yes, that's right, Kirk. Just who is he?" She listened to his reply and all the time her eyes kept flicking behind her.

"I see, a general and he comes from the Foreign Office. No, he wouldn't tell me what he wanted. Not to you either? Goodbye, Tom." She pressed down the receiver, then made another call.

"Operator," she said. "I want a long distance number please. Yes, to Minechester." Her voice was still controlled and quite without accent, but something was happening to her face.

CHAPTER TWELVE

"And I still think he's crazy." Michael ground his cigarette into the already overflowing ash-tray and scowled at the notes in front of him.

"I've every respect for the old man, but this is going a bit too far. What the hell does he think he's up to? He disregards everything that I tell him and which the police agree with and goes on about some vague occult rigmarole. Finally he sends me off on two quite ridiculous wild goose chases. Just look at them for yourself."

"Thank you," Penny crossed the room and sat on the arm of his chair. She smiled slightly as she looked at the notes he had taken down.

"Now, let's see. Yes, my sweet, you're in for an instructive afternoon it seems. Firstly, you are to visit the borough engineer and from him take copious details of all the buildings in the area of the river steps; that should keep you pretty busy. Then what?" She turned a page and her smile changed to a wide grin.

"Ahah, this will be nice. He wants a full list of all religious societies in the district which can be described as being of an unorthodox or eccentric nature. Yes, I think you're in for a hard time, my dear; there will probably be scores of them. Finally, you are to meet him at the station at eleven o'clock, bringing with you a full account of your labors. Still, bear up and remember how it goes. 'The trivial round, the common task should furnish all we need to ask.'"

"Oh, shut up, girl, and stop laughing. As I said, I don't know what he thinks he's up to." Michael pushed the papers to one side and walked to the window. Across the roof of the building opposite, he could see the tall bridge with a train pluming its way to the south. He wished very much that he was on it.

"Surely, now we know that this girl was not Gerda Raine and

the Russians had nothing to do with it, he realizes it is no longer our business. It has nothing to do with us at all. She may have looked like her and worn her ring, but so what! She could have got the ring in a hundred different ways and this is the work of the police. When he left, he put me in sole charge of the department, and what am I doing; making lists of decayed buildings and indexing the local religious nuts."

"Cheer up, Mike. I'm rather with him, you know. I'd hate to leave this case now even if it is not really our affair. Remember, he said he was going to break it in the morning."

"Yes, he said that, but can he? I rather doubt it. As far as I can see, we're no farther forward at all; except to know that it has nothing at all to do with us. I'm beginning to feel that this may go on for days and he's using it for an excuse to keep away from his blasted grouse moor." He turned from the window and looked at her. Suddenly a slight trace of humor came into his face.

"Well, now," he said. "You've enjoyed seeing my worksheet, but just look at your own. I think you're in for a thoroughly good time as well. Go on, turn the page and look at it." He watched her read on and felt a little better as her grin turned to an expression of annoyance.

"But damn it. Who does Kirk think he is? After all I'm merely a fellow-traveler of your department. I've already been bored to tears by that ass Peter Brett and now I've got to try and make a date with him.

"He'll tell us nothing, as well. I'm quite sure of that; far too interested in his own literary genius to notice anyone who wasn't sitting at his feet admiring him. Very well, let's see what I'm supposed to do." She flicked over the pages and read on. Then she got up and went to the telephone.

"I see. I have to ring friend Brett and ask him to have a meal with me. I must tell him that the case is closed and chat socially to him; playing the little pony-tailed art follower I suppose. Wherever possible, I must bring the conversation round to the murdered girl and his relationship with her. A very pleasant social evening this should be; slightly sinister as well. He adds that on no account must I allow Brett to take me anywhere not frequented by the general public. I am to leave him at ten forty-five and join you at the station. Well, it's after two now; if I'm going to give our beautiful friend time to prepare, I suppose I'd better ring him."

She picked up the directory and ran her finger down the pages. Just as she found the number, the phone rang at her side.

"Hullo, yes, this is Mrs. Wise. Who is that speaking? Oh, I see." She glanced back at Michael and her expression was quite bewildered.

"But this is most extraordinary," she said into the phone. "As a matter of fact I was going to ring you myself; yes, this very minute. But of course, I'd love to. That was what I was going to ask you. We're off to town in the morning and I'd so much like to see you before I go.

"Where shall we say then? Oh, I see. Wouldn't it be better if I met you at the restaurant? Oh, very well, you'll pick me up in a taxi then. All right, seven sharp and I'm looking forward to it. I'm afraid I can't dress up much as I've hardly anything with me. Goodbye till I see you."

She replaced the phone and frowned at Michael. "Well, you can guess who that was; Brett himself. It's strange isn't it? Almost like, '*talk of the devil.*' He contacts me a second before I ring him. I can't understand it, Mike, but I'm beginning to feel that the old man may be on to something. It's almost as if he knew that Brett would call and wanted to prepare me for it. I'm not sure I like it, you know."

"No, neither do I." Michael took up Kirk's notes and ran through them.

"Now, listen, Penny. I think you may be right and Kirk will break this case, but I'm still worried. It's just possible that friend Brett may be a little brighter than he seems, so be careful. Remember your orders. Do not be alone with him anywhere.

"Now, I'd better get along and meet my pal the sanitary-inspector. Look after yourself and see you at the station." He smiled at her for a moment and then leaned forward and kissed her.

"Remember, sweet. Don't be alone with him anywhere."

He turned and walked out of the door, leaving her to prepare for a date which would quite probably kill her.

There was something wrong with Peter Brett. Even before the revolving door had swept behind him Penny sensed it, though it was nothing visible; nothing in his waved hair, his dark suit or his studied smile. He looked exactly as he had done before, tall, handsome and false, but it was there and it came in front of him as he crossed the hall towards her. It was like an odor, an atmosphere, a shadow that moved with him and it was all quite wrong.

"My dear Mrs. Wise," he said, "this is delightful, really delightful." He smiled at her through his mass of atmosphere and ran an admiring eye over her sack-line dress.

"And how very nice you look. Usually I disapprove so strongly of those things, but on you it seems quite perfect; I'm afraid a lot of our local noses are going to be put sadly out of joint this evening. No, no, let's not have a drink here, this place depresses me terribly." He waved an approaching waiter aside.

"By the way, I don't even know your first name. Penny. Penny Wise! What fun. I'll be Pound Foolish. Well, Penny, shall we go? I've left a cab outside and the constabulary are dead hot on parking offenses, if not on detecting murders." He took her arm and led her out of the dark hall to the door.

The taxi was waiting at the foot of the steps and it was a black Morris saloon with a uniformed driver sitting in it. He looked a small frail man and it took him all his time to lean round and pull open the door. Brett stood back for Penny and then climbed in and settled himself beside her.

He smiled at her under the little roof light but somehow the atmosphere he carried blanketed out his smile and made it meaningless.

"I'm afraid it's a terrible place I'm taking you to, but there's really nothing else in this town. It used to be the haunt of the local potentates; iron-master, ship-owners and so on, but that's all gone with 'Thebes the Golden,' I fear. Now it's packed with workingmen staggering under their bulging pay-pockets. Tell me though, you said on the phone that you were going back to London tomorrow. Does that mean that this wretched business is wrapped up at last?"

"Yes, as far as we're concerned, it's finished." Just as Kirk had ordered, Penny told him everything. She told him about Michael and the death of Mrs. Carlton and the removal of her body, and the certainty of the police that if they got Carlton they would have the answer to everything.

"Yes, as far as we're concerned, it's over. We know that the murdered girl wasn't Gerda Raine, and that lets us out. We're quite satisfied on that score and it's all up to the police now. They shouldn't have much trouble in tracing Carlton, I imagine. Remember, he was carrying a dead woman with him."

"Yes, his mother's body. Poor, poor, devil; I feel terribly sorry for him, even if he did kill Gladys and lay out your friend Howard. Besides it means that you will be leaving us. A pity that, I feel that we could have got on so well together you know. A great pity, Penny Wise." He bent over towards her and his hand rested on her knee and moved upwards a fraction.

Penny didn't even bother to brush it off or tighten her legs. There was no need. Under his dashing manner, his smile, his nice clothes and—yes—his quite real charm, there was something soft about Brett; soft and asexual and at the same time terribly pathetic. She felt less threat or excitement from his touch than she would have done from a child's. She grinned at him and then pulled her coat around her as the cab drew up outside a restaurant.

Cherry's Bar, Grill and Dance Hall had once catered for the cream of Minechester society, but that was a long time ago. Now, it was crowded, raucous and rather jolly. It had an American bar at the back, a line of alcoves for those who wanted privacy and a big dance floor with a band. It wasn't a very good band perhaps, but it made a great deal of noise. Though she knew she must keep her mind on the job, Penny fancied she might be going to enjoy herself.

She didn't. The evening went just like that sort of evening

always does, but there was no fun or gaiety in it. They ate a little, danced a little and drank a lot, but it wouldn't work. All the time, Brett's atmosphere was too close around her, swamping out joy.

He flirted with her, smiled at her, stroked her hand and held her very close when they were dancing, but it didn't mean a thing. He didn't want her as a woman, he couldn't have cared less about her as a woman. If she had been lying in front of him, naked on black sheets, he wouldn't have wanted her; least of all that way, probably. She wasn't a person to him, so much as part of a game he was playing. He was the provincial Casanova, the Baudelaire, the young Byron and it was all a game. There was only one woman in his life who could move him, and that was his mother. All the other women were just toys to boost up his ego, to play with up to a point and—she looked up at the blue eyes above her—finally to humiliate and work out some form of revenge for his barren life.

"Yes, there was only one woman for Peter Brett." She stiffened slightly in his arms as a thought came to her. One woman and yet too many women. There had been too many women and far too many mothers in this case. From the start there had been too many. Mrs. Carlton, who even in death had stayed with her son. The formidable creature with her crushed maid, her unpaying-guest and the son who played the pianola. And Mrs. Brett too. Mrs. Brett with this man, so dashing, so gay, so much the lady-killer, the creative genius but all the time without love or energy. Three women with their dead. What was it Browning had said? "Poor man he lived another sort of life in that new-stuccoed third house on the bridge." Penny's eyes were very thoughtful as the music died and he led her back to the table. She put all thought of pleasure out of her mind and prepared to concentrate on the job in hand.

Kirk's orders were quite definite. He wanted to know what, if any, had been the relationship between Brett and the murdered girl and that was all Penny had to find out. She had to talk to Peter Brett and make him tell her the answer to that one question.

She did her best. She laughed at his jokes, held his hand and allowed him to press her foot beneath the table. Now and then, occasionally, very occasionally, she slipped in a question.

"I'm sure Gladys must have been fond of you." "Did you ever take her out?" "Did you make a pass at her?"

And it all got her nowhere. He listened to her, answered her questions and told her nothing at all. Before they had reached the second course, she was sure that Kirk was wrong and there was nothing to be learnt from Peter Brett. And gradually she saw something else. Behind his personality and his weakness, she sensed something that was not at all weak. Suddenly she knew that it was not she who was doing the watching and not Brett either. There was another person behind him who was using his eyes to look at her. As she looked at his eyes, Kirk's instructions seemed quite trivial and a theory of her own started to grow.

"Tell me, Peter," she said, "it's rude of me to ask, I know, but I'm interested in my friends. Who was your father?"

"He was nobody, sweetie, just a doctor. He practiced abroad and I remember very little about him. He—died." For the third time she heard the pause between the words and they were just words, as if death itself were self-explanatory. Not, "he died of malaria," or "he died when I was a child." Just, "he died."

"We lived with an uncle of mine after that. He was in the regular army and one of the most foolish men I have ever met. Still, there is nothing very remarkable about our family; just my future. You're not drinking though." He smiled and pushed the glass towards her with his hand curved over the rim. And as she looked at him and drank and smiled back, she seemed to see him clearly for the first time. Somehow he reminded her of someone she had once known slightly and forgotten. It was only there for a second and then he was just Mrs. Brett's boy standing up in front of her.

"Come on," he said, "let's dance again." He gave her the studied smile as he said it and taking her arm, led her out onto the floor.

The band was playing an American version of a Scottish university song and they gave it all they had; the saxophonist looked like a bursting red flower on a black and white stalk as he swayed on the edge of the stage. Brett held her very tightly in his arms with his lips touching her hair as he crooned the words. *"I'm a rambling wreck from Georgia Tech and a hell of an engineer—"*

She could feel his breath on her scalp and his fingers were gently caressing the fold of her back, but he didn't care about her; he couldn't have cared less. For everything he said or did, he was as indifferent to her as if he had been a gigolo dancing with a brewer's two-hundred-pound, middle-aged, nymphomaniac widow. There was a great sadness in Penny's eyes as she danced with him, for he was all negation. He was the beaten man, the mum's boy, the always talker and the never doer. The real genuine hurter because he had nothing to give or even to take. The saxophone screamed out the tune and the voice in her hair ran softly on.

"A helluva—helluva—helluva—helluva—hell of an engineer—"

And all at once, she knew who it was that Brett reminded her of. It wasn't a person at all; just a photograph. A photograph she had once looked at in Kirk's office, while she handed her passport to a little, bitter and very confident girl who quoted Napoleon. Another hell of an engineer. A captain of Royal Engineers who had lost everything for love and had not even been left with the strength to kill himself decently. As she listened to the words, she knew quite clearly why Gerda Raine or her substitute had died.

"Like every decent fellow, I drink my whisky clear—"

Yes, like every decent fellow, you drink and act as you have to. She twisted farther round in his arms and as she studied that handsome, somehow unhandsome face, she saw that it was the same. The same face that had blown itself to bits, and all for the love of a lady. She was sure of everything when at last the music crashed to crescendo and faded.

"I'm a rambling wreck from Georgia Tech and a hell of an engineer."

"Peter," she said. "That uncle you lived with? I think I can guess his name, you know. It was Richmond, wasn't it, Captain Hugh Richmond?"

Brett didn't answer her. He just looked at her with his unchanged smile and he didn't let her go as the band stopped playing. It was a good thing he didn't, because as Penny stood in his arms the room started to go round. It swung round to the left and back again and it was on springs and hinges and it looked quite different.

She clutched hard against him, forcing herself to stand upright in that swinging room and slowly his face became different, too. It seemed to contract; the flesh left it, the smile left it and it became hard and efficient and quite without expression. As she watched him, it seemed to Penny that the only point of focus in the world was that hard expressionless face.

"Come on, my dear," he said. "You're going to be all right, but you're sick now, aren't you. I'm afraid I had to make you sick, so I put something in your glass. Don't worry about it, it won't hurt you. You see, my mother's name was Richmond and we have to have a little talk about it. Come on, Penny, you're very ill, so come back to the table and there will be someone there to help you." She walked back with him, leaning on his arm, and there was somebody at the table. Somebody was a big woman in a tight dress that wasn't quite respectable. She had shiny boots that almost came up to her knees and there was a port-wine mark down the side of her face. It creased slightly as she smiled at Penny. It was a nice friendly smile and she looked comforting and maternal.

"Hullo, dearie," she said. "You're feeling poorly, aren't you? Don't worry about it though, pet. Just you come along with me and I'll see you are all right. Come on, dear, come with Connie; old Connie knows what to do with you." She put an arm round her shoulder and led her to a door at the back of the hall. "That's right, don't worry about anything. We'll go and bathe your face with some nice cold water and everything will be fine again."

And Penny went with her. She wanted to go with her, for this woman was security; the only firm and settled thing left on Earth. She leaned against her as they went through the door and she had never known anything more warm and comforting and free from fear as the salty smell of her big body.

The Ladies' Room was at the end of the passage where another door led out into a yard. It was bright with green tiles and washbasins and there was a row of cubicles at the back. Penny let go the woman's arm and staggered to the nearest basin, filling it and sluicing water onto her face. Almost at once her head cleared and the room stopped swinging sideways.

"Well, that's better, isn't it?" Connie smiled at her again and then turned to the door and shot the bolt across it.

"Yes, much better. You'll be quite all right in a minute, but we'll wait a bit and not have anybody coming in to disturb you. Now, dry your face, dear, and comb your hair. That's right, Mrs. Wise, look at yourself in the mirror." The voice became a little harder as she spoke her name.

Penny never heard the altered tone. She wiped the water from her face and she breathed deeply for a moment. She felt quite safe and warm and at home. Then she looked up into the mirror and she had never felt colder in her life.

The room was quite still now and everything was back to normal; the light glistened on the tiles and far away she could hear the band playing. Everything was back to normal except the mirror; and the mirror was lying.

Penny looked in the mirror and it had two faces; they were both hers. She stood quite still and looked at her faces and, as she looked, the drug took hold of her again and the room started to sway.

The faces in the mirror stared back at her and they were almost identical. The one on the left was weak and bewildered and its lips moved as hers did, but the other face was hers too. It had the same hair style, the same coloring, the same make-up and even the little mole on her left cheek.

Very slowly, Penny turned and looked at the woman who had come out of the cubicle behind her and wore her face. Just before the room went black she heard her speak.

"Hullo, Mrs. Wise," said Gerda Raine.

CHAPTER THIRTEEN

Steam, grit and fog. A rattle of trolleys and empty milk-cans, a long sigh from the waiting locomotive and a hoarse voice whispering information on the Tannoy; the North-Western Station at ten forty-five.

Michael Howard walked slowly across the booking-hall and

looked round for Penny. There was no sign of her. He crossed to the arrival platforms and glanced up at the chalked notice-board. Kirk would be late, very late. As he read the message, the loudspeaker above his head growled its confirmation. "Owing to repairs on the line, the eleven four train from London is running twenty-five minutes late. It will arrive at platform two at twenty-nine minutes past eleven."

Michael looked at the clock, hitched his coat around his shoulders and with a final glance round the station to see if Penny had arrived, walked across to the buffet.

As he had half expected it was shut. There was a chain and a forbidding notice across the door and through the glass, a turkey-cock face frowned and shook its head at him. He grinned at it, salaamed, and moving to a trolley, bought a cup of very sweet, quite cold coffee. Then he sat down on a bench and opening his brief-case, prepared to make a final check of the notes he had brought for Kirk.

They were all there, all he had been told to do and none of them made the slightest sense to him. He had a neat list of all the more lunatic religious groups in the area and there were plenty of them. They ranged from neo-fascism to vague beliefs in levitation and he couldn't see why any of them should be of interest.

He turned over three pages and looked at his next heading. "Subject; All buildings, drains and underground works in the vicinity of the River Steps Minechester." He had them all; houses, warehouses, connections to the sewers and even an old shaft which had once led from a disused factory to the water. He shook his head sadly at his chief's eccentricity and lighting a cigarette, once more looked up for Penny. There was no sign of her and the hands of the station clock stood at three minutes to the hour. He had no feeling of anxiety yet, but he was starting to grow curious. She had many faults, but time-keeping had never been one of them. As he looked at the clock, the speaker above it burst into life.

"Will Mr. Michael Howard please call at the Station Master's office. Mr. Michael Howard to the Station Master's office at once please."

He put down his paper cup and hurried across the hall to a door under the bridge. It had a green notice with Station Master outside and inside there was a table with a very fat man sitting behind it. He held a telephone in one hand and a steaming cup of tea in the other. He grinned as Michael came in but he didn't bother to get up.

"Name of 'Oward? Good. Telephone call for you. The young lady says it's urgent; matter of the 'ighest importance. Still, I wouldn't worry if I were you, knowing women. Got one of my own at home." He shook his head sadly and pushed the phone across the table to Michael.

"Hullo, hullo, is that you, Mike? Oh, thank goodness I've caught you." Penny's voice was quick and sounded oddly breathless, as if she had been running.

"Look, Mike, I've got it. Yes, I know everything, the lot, I know exactly what killed that girl and where Mrs. Carlton is. It's all wrapped up but you must come to me at once." She broke off and there was silence on the line.

"Hullo, Penny. Are you there? Please go on, just what have you found out?"

"Listen, Mike, you must come at once." There was no answer to his question, not even a hint there had been a break in the conversation. It was just a flow of words.

"You must come now, Mike. If you do, we can finish the business tonight. I've sent a taxi for you. It's a black Morris and the driver knows where to find me. It will be parked at the far end of the station, waiting for you. Please, please don't argue, Mike, just do as I say. Never mind about the General. It won't take long, just a few minutes and then the case will be broken. You will come, won't you, Mike? Please, promise me that you'll come."

"But listen, Penny, you must let me know more. Just tell me what you've found out first." His voice was very tense and urgent but it did no good, her words ran on as if she had never heard him.

"Please, please, promise me you'll come, Mike. Please tell me that you'll come."

"Very well, I'll promise," he said, and the same moment he

heard the click as the line went dead. He dropped the phone back into its rest and stood quite still.

"Well, everything all right, chum?" The fat man put a cigarette into his mouth and somehow he managed to smile and talk as he lit it.

"No, everything is not all right." Michael looked up at the clock at the back of the room and tried to think.

Everything was not all right, and that was the understatement of all time. Everything was damn wrong. It wasn't Penny's voice, her breathlessness or excitement, her refusal to listen to him. It wasn't the fact that she had no right to ask him to disobey Kirk. If she really was on to something, she might have thought it was worth-while. It was something much smaller that was so terribly wrong. Kirk himself. "The general." Neither of them had ever called him that. "The old man," "Kirk," even "General Kirk," but never "the General." As he considered that one little slip, he knew that though it might have been Penny's voice on the line it was not her mind behind it. He stared once more at the clock, thought hard and decided.

It wasn't a matter of thought or duty any more but he had to go to her. Purely out of personal emotion, he would go to her. Wherever she was, safe or in danger he would go to her. He tore a leaf from his pocket-book, scrawled a note and turned to the man at the table.

"Look," he said. "I'm in a bit of trouble and I want to ask you a favor. I'm supposed to be meeting a man off the London train, but something has cropped up and I can't make it. Yes, that's right, the one that comes in at twenty-five past. I want you to meet him for me and give him a message."

"Now, don't you bother your head about that, chum, I'll catch him all right. Get him on the speaker for you. Easy as falling off a log."

"No, I'm afraid that wouldn't do. This man is very shy and he wouldn't like hearing his name called out. I want you to meet him personally when he comes through the barrier."

"Ho, no, sorry, chum, but that won't do. Like to help, of course, but it's out of the question, right out. There's only me and old Charlie on tonight and Charlie's not too hot with the phone." He tapped his head significantly and winked.

"Very down on officials leaving their posts, the station master is. Very strict where regulations are concerned. Very keen on having a really trustworthy man on the blower. Why, chum, I wouldn't leave this room if you was to offer me arf a nicker. Very strict indeed the station master is . . ." Once more came the call to duty and then his voice trailed off as Michael opened his wallet and laid a green note on the table.

"Well, of course, sir, seeing that it really seems to be an emergency, I suppose I must make an exception to the rules for once. Made to be broken, I think someone once said. Besides, I like to help me fellow men; can't help it, it's just that I'm made that way. Charlie!" As he raised his voice his hand flicked out and the note vanished. A moment later, the door at the back of the room opened and a bent, wizened and incredibly aged figure stood blinking in the light.

"Charlie, a bit of bother has cropped up and you'll have to hold the fort for a while. I know I can rely on you. Now, sir, seeing it's you, I'll meet your friend for you. Just let's have his name and what he looks like."

With great detail Michael described Kirk; then he handed him the leaf from his pocket, looked at the clock and walked out. It was five minutes past the hour.

Outside the station it was quite dark. The mist that had drifted in from the sea was turning to rain and, even in the shelter of the portico, he felt a few drops on his face. He pulled down his hat, turned up his collar and walked quickly towards the parking lot.

He found it quite easily. It was a cinder-strewn bomb-site under the side of the embankment and there were no more than a dozen cars standing in it. Only one of them had lights.

Right at the end of the line there was a large black Morris of pre-war vintage with its lamps glowing in the rain and the shadow of a uniformed cap above the wheel. Michael walked towards it and bent down to speak to the driver. Just before he saw his face, the door at the back opened and a voice spoke to him.

"Mr. Howard, will you get in please. Yes, I would like you to sit beside me." It was a warm voice which could best be described as cozy; it had a ring of road-houses, Brighton hotels and one-night-bedrooms.

Michael turned and looked at her through the open door. She was a slim middle-aged woman whom he had never seen before. She was smiling and she held something in her hand. She turned on the light so that he could see what she held. It was a child's toy.

"Get in please, Mr. Howard. Your friend Mrs. Wise is most anxious to see you. She told me to ask you to hurry." The voice lowered a little, but it was still warm and friendly.

"Please get in. I've no wish to hurt you, you know, but believe me, I can. I can hurt you a great deal."

Michael looked at the thing in her hand and his world started to go round. It was a child's water pistol and it might have cost five and sixpence. It was made of yellow-painted metal and there was "Super-Chief" emblazoned on the barrel. It looked quite silly as she held it, but as he looked at her face, he knew what it would contain. It was full of vitriol, sulphuric acid, and it could be the last thing he would ever see. Let him hesitate another second and he would never see anything again and nobody would look at him without shuddering. In that little toy were the two things he dreaded in life. Without another word, Michael Howard, that strong, hard and very ruthless man, got in and sat down beside the woman with her child's toy.

"Thank you, Mr. Howard. Now will you please close the door and be very careful how you do it? That's right, keep your face towards me." As the door swung to, her left hand came forward and there was a sharp pain in his arm. Just before his eyes closed he saw the driver's face. It was James Carlton and the clock in front of him showed ten minutes past eleven.

Through the night, the long train that was bringing Kirk, hurried to make up lost time; but it was already five miles, eight minutes and an eternity too late.

CHAPTER FOURTEEN

"Thank you, Mrs. Wise, that was good and clear and I think it will bring him." Mrs. Brett put down the telephone and switched off the tape-recorder. Then she sat down and smiled at Penny. Her smile was very white and friendly and attractive but it wasn't human at all.

"A wonderful invention the tape-recorder, quite wonderful. I have not the slightest idea how it works, but we couldn't have done without it. Probably we would have had to hurt you a great deal and I do dislike pain; even in others. It was such a good thing that we could get you to talk under the drug. Oh, I'm sorry, I'd forgotten. You poor thing, you must be suffocating." Her very white, soft and beautifully manicured hand reached out and gently pulled the sticking-plaster from Penny's mouth.

"Now, that's better isn't it? Soon you'll be feeling quite yourself again."

Penny didn't answer her. The drug Brett had given her was still strong and her body seemed to be held in a mass of tightly packed cotton-wool. But stronger than the drug and far worse, there was bewilderment and fear; terrible fear. For as she looked at the woman's cool, smiling and friendly face she saw that it was just a mask and behind it lay the worst thing in the world.

"Who are you?" she asked. "I know your name, I know where you live, I know your son drugged me, but who are you?"

"But I thought that you had guessed that, Mrs. Wise. I heard that when you were dancing with my son you told him who I was. Have you forgotten so soon, my dear?" As remembrance came into Penny's face, her smile widened a little.

"Yes, that's quite right, my name was Richmond, Sarah Richmond, and I once had a brother. I had a very dear brother, but somebody took him away from me. You remember now, don't you; you remember Hugh Richmond, Mrs. Wise?" She took a photograph from the table at her side and held it out to Penny. It showed a Georgian house with wide lawns and flower beds and there were three people standing in front of the door. One was Peter Brett as a child, one was herself and the other looked like Peter Brett as he was now. He wore an army lieutenant's uniform and Penny could just make out the "R.E." flashes on the lapels. They could have been any happy family group.

"Yes, Hugh Richmond was my brother and I was very fond of him. It's so strange that nobody should have guessed the connection before. Everyone seems to have been on the wrong track from the beginning. The police, with their absurd theory of a homicidal maniac; poor James Carlton, who never harmed a fly. Your rather silly superior, General Kirk, who seemed to think it was some kind of Russian plot and came to me posing as a minor official of the Immigration Office.

"Oh, yes, Mrs. Wise, I know who Kirk is. Shall we say, a little bird told me; a little bird whom I killed. It's so strange that nobody had the least understanding of why she was killed; that there was only one person with a really valid reason for killing Gerda Raine."

"Gerda Raine!" Penny's mind fought against the fumes of the drug and the fumes of her fear and she was back in the Ladies' Room of Cherry's Bar, Grill and Restaurant with a woman watching her from a bolted door and the face that looked like her face in the mirror.

"But you didn't kill Gerda Raine, you couldn't have killed her. I saw her tonight. Besides, she wasn't the girl in the river. Kirk knew that, he got it from the Russians. You haven't killed her, she's still alive."

"Is she, Mrs. Wise? Is she really alive, I wonder. It seems to me that I did kill her, you know."

The smile went off her face and for a moment, Penny looked at the thing behind the mask. It was only there for a tenth of a second as if she was seeing it through a camera shutter, but it was enough. As she looked through that cool, civilized face, she knew that whatever she had imagined before would be nothing before the reality.

"How many times can a person die, Mrs. Wise? How many ways are there of killing a person? Some of them are obvious of course; the rope, the bullet, or perhaps a seven inch carving knife. There are others though and I am going to show you one of them, my dear. Just look at the door on your left and then tell me if I haven't killed Gerda Raine." She lifted her hands from her sides and brought them together with a sharp clap.

Penny turned and looked at the door. It was at the end of the long room which seemed to have no windows or furniture and was lit by a single, staring light bulb without a shade. Mrs. Brett's hands had scarcely separated when the door opened and she understood.

Gerda Raine came slowly into the room and her face had no expression at all. She wore the same make-up as Penny, the same hair style and Penny's coat was around her shoulders; at a first glance she looked quite like her, but it was just a trick, an illusion. She didn't look like anybody at all.

That was the secret, she was nobody and she could be taken for anybody. Her face was so dead, so without life, that given the right size, the right clothes and the right coloring she could have been anybody at all; if you didn't look too closely.

Penny did. She looked at the face through the powder and she knew what she was looking at. It was the same face that had smiled at her in Kirk's gloomy office, but it had been changed. The girl in the doorway was an imbecile.

"Well, Mrs. Wise, now do you understand? Can you still tell me that I didn't kill her?" Mrs. Brett clapped her hands again and the creature turned automatically and went out of the room as silently as she had come.

"Yes, I understand now." Penny braced herself against her chair and prepared to spring forward. She had no words to say to the woman; there was nothing left to say. All she could do was to kill her; kill her quickly, as though she were destroying a poisonous insect.

Her spring never came. As she started to get up, there was a sudden jerk at her waist and she was pulled back. She looked down and saw that she was fastened to the wall behind her by a thin steel chain.

"How could I bring myself to do such a thing? That's what you want to ask me, isn't it, my dear? Among the sentimental there is always a horror about the insane. The fact that I have made that creature what she is shocks you doesn't it? Believe me though, I had a reason." Her voice rose slightly and Penny knew that if Gerda Raine's mind had gone, this woman's was dead too and filled by something which had nothing to do with humanity.

"Let me tell you a story and then perhaps you may understand my reason." Mrs. Brett lit a cigarette and settled herself down on the only other chair in the room with her legs crossed. She had rather lovely legs for her age and wore very sheer stockings.

"There was once a girl, my dear, who loved too much; far too much perhaps, but she couldn't help it. She got married when she was very young and for a time she was happy with the man she married. Then that man changed; he withered and later he died. He died very horribly of drink, drugs and an unmentionable disease. He died because he met a woman like the creature I have just shown you. A little poisonous creature who had one aim in life and only one; the destruction of things that did not belong to her. A woman like Gerda Raine.

"When her man died, that woman's life crashed around her with him, but she hung on. She had a child to protect and something else; you might call it faith. She had been living in a very out-of-the-way part of the world and she found something that comforted her. When she came back to England, she brought her comfort with her. If you look over there, you can see the symbol of that comfort."

Penny followed her pointing finger and all at once she began to understand what Kirk had muttered to her in the car. Nailed to the far wall of the room there was a wooden carving. It showed the figure of a boy, almost a child, and it had oddly distorted joints.

"The woman came back to this country and she tried to build her life again. She still remembered her husband though, and sometimes she talked to other women about him and told them why he had died. Sometimes she met women who understood and she made friends; lots of friends. Women like herself who had all been hurt by male weakness and female wickedness.

"In time she told her friends about the faith she had found, and because many of them had something they loved and wanted to protect they joined her in it. They made a pact together. A pact that they would work and fight and if necessary die together to protect what they had left to them.

"Now, do you understand a little of my story, Mrs. Wise?"

And Penny did understand. She understood quite clearly. A band of women; women with sons, who had been forsaken or betrayed by their husbands. Dominating women who would stop at nothing to keep the affection of those sons. Lots of women; the Bretts, the Carltons, the woman with the terrible mouth and the old tart in the Ladies' Room at the restaurant. And perhaps a hundred others; an organization bounded and united by that broken symbol on the wall. She felt quite cold and helpless as she looked at it with its twisted limbs and flat blind eyes.

"Yes, I understand," she said. "And because of your brother—"

"Yes, because of my brother, Mrs. Wise. My brother who was one of the finest men I have ever known, but because of a little go-getting girl called Gerda Raine was not even left with the strength to kill himself decently." She looked up for a moment and as her face came under the arc of the light, Penny saw that there was a tear on her cheek. It looked quite out of place and slightly indecent on her cold face.

"After that, I and my friends decided to act. It took us a long time and a great deal of trouble, but at last we found her. After that it was easy. My son made friends with her and she was brought to this city in much the same way as you were brought here. Then things were done to her. I am rather proud of those things we did.

"You must understand, Mrs. Wise, that in her case, death was not enough; not nearly enough for what she had done. We had to maim her. My husband was a doctor and I had learned a little from him before he went to pieces. It was all quite simple. Given the right amount of a certain drug and a single note from a piano played over and over and over again, even a little hard mind like hers will soon go empty."

"I see. It was done at the house of your friend, wasn't it?" Even through her horror, Penny saw how it was done. She could picture the doped girl stretched out on the couch and a boy with small hands sitting before a pianola with his legs working on the pedals and a single note rose and fell around them. While under its blows the girl's mind withered.

"Yes, at the house of Mrs. Travers, my very good friend; Mrs. Travers who has also suffered as I have done. As all of us have done in one way or another. She took Gerda for two weeks and at the end of those weeks she became as she is now, just an automaton."

"Yes, I understand that, but the other girl, the one who really died, who was she and what had she done to deserve the death you gave her?"

"She was a thief." Mrs. Travers, whom she had not noticed before, moved forward and stood in front of Penny. Her thin mouth was slightly open, showing the line of her teeth.

"She was my lodger and she tried to take something that belonged to me." Her words came slowly with a great intensity behind them and as she looked at that set face, Penny knew what it was the girl had tried to steal.

"Your son?"

"Yes, my son, Mrs. Wise. The one thing I have left to love in my life and she tried to take him away from me. She came to my house six months ago. She had no relations or friends and because I was sorry for her I gave her a room. Soon she started to repay me." She broke off for a moment and wiped her mouth with the sleeve of her blouse.

"Yes, she was going to take him away. They used to talk about music and I never guessed what she really wanted. She told him that she had saved a little money and they could take a flat together. She said that even though his hands were deformed, he could get some kind of a job. She said she loved him. Love; as if a creature like that could begin to understand the meaning of the word.

"I spoke to Mrs. Brett about it and then we started to act. She looked very like Gerda, you see, and it was easy. I talked to my son and made him understand what she really was; a little evil creature who wanted to destroy him and me. She took the drug from him quite without any suspicion when he gave her a cup of coffee. Then we killed her.

"You do see that we had to kill her, don't you, Mrs. Wise?" There was an odd note of appeal in her voice as if Penny's understanding was somehow important to her.

"Would you like me to tell you just how we did it?"

Penny shook her head. There was no need for her to know any more. She knew all the details now and it was quite clear. Just given the possibility of this gang of injured embittered women with their sons to help them and everything fitted; if they had Gerda Raine as well. A purely automatic tool who resembled the girl they were going to kill.

It was Gerda who had gone to the "Castle," of course. Gerda Raine with her controller beside her; a haggard woman who didn't look very respectable. It was she who was on the bus with Carlton and had gone with him to the river steps. And there he would have left her, just as he said he had, while two reliable witnesses walked up the steps to collaborate his quite true story.

Then they would have passed by and somebody would have come out of the house to collect her because she had no will or mind to act independently. And lower down, at the foot of the steps the real story would be taking place. The real victim would be ready and waiting, doped and stupid and dressed like Gerda with her ring on her finger till the clock struck, the tug-boat churned round the bend of the river and Mrs. Travers came out of the shadow with her knife.

It was neat and simple and it all fitted together perfectly. You had all your witnesses as to time, place and identity; even in the bar you had them, where a stout whore with a port-wine mark on her face was ready to identify the girl with Carlton and the time he took her out.

There was only one factor that they hadn't checked and he didn't matter now. Rouse, the husband of Mrs. Carlton who had become a lodger at the house where Gerda was taken. Rouse who had seen the drugged maid which was Gerda's disguise and guessed the link between the women. Rouse who had died because his wife was no longer a person at all but just a servant of the thing she had followed.

Penny looked up at the figure on the wall and for the first time she seemed to see it as it really was; not a talisman or a symbol, but a god; a god in the kingdom of pain and the woman in front of it was its prophet.

She moved her body against the chain, but it was very strong and tight and there was no release from it.

"No," she said. "I don't want to know how you killed that girl, I just want to know why you have brought me here and told me all this?"

"I see. Can't you guess, my dear?" It was Mrs. Brett who answered. "General Kirk hasn't told you then. It appears he fancies that he knows something. He called on a person in London and asked her some questions. What he didn't know is that that person is one of us and she has spoken to me on the telephone. I have now to prepare for his return.

"You see, the police know nothing and we have no fears from them. All we fear is Kirk, so he will have to go. I am very sorry, Mrs. Wise, but you are the way that he will go.

"We have nothing against you, Mrs. Wise, but you are to be our tool; you and Mr. Howard. By now, I imagine that Mr. Howard will have followed the instructions of your very clear recording and be on his way here. When he arrives, my friends will come and we will start to prepare. I think I know the way it will be done." She was like a business woman planning a routine action.

"When General Kirk gets off the train and finds nobody to meet him, he will go to the hotel or the police station. In either case there will be a note waiting for him. It will be in Mr. Howard's handwriting and it will ask him to go to a certain place at a certain time. If I have read Kirk's character correctly, he will say nothing to the police but go there alone." She broke off for a moment as footsteps sounded outside the door.

"Yes, that should be Mr. Howard now, I imagine. It is almost time for us to start.

"Oh, I'm sorry, my dear, I forgot to finish what I was saying. When Kirk gets to the place of meeting, the three of you, you and Mr. Howard and Gerda Raine: you are going to kill him."

Once more she smiled her sad smile at Penny and then turned her head. Behind her the door opened and Michael Howard, the only man that Penny had ever loved, wanted or cared about, crawled into the room on his knees.

CHAPTER FIFTEEN

Pacific locomotive 8302 "Red Knight" crossed the home points at seventy miles an hour with her cut-out and regulator wide. She had always been a good time-keeper and she was struggling to make up the lost half hour. Not till she approached the long down slope into Minechester did her driver's hand leave the throttle.

Kirk sat by himself in a first-class pullman compartment with a glass of Bass in front of him and he appeared deeply engrossed in a back issue of "Ruff's Guide to the Turf." Not till the train's motion changed from a clicking rush to a checked gallop did he look up. He glanced out at the shadowy beginnings of the town and pushed the "Ruff" into his brief case. Then he put on his coat and his hands ran over two objects in the pockets.

If any of his fellow passengers had seen what he carried, they would have been surprised. One was a thin folder of safe-breaker's tools and the other an Enfield revolver. It was a small elderly gun of six chambers and twenty-two calibre and it didn't look very effective. It was. The cone of each bullet had been carefully drilled and on meeting the least resistance of bone or muscle would fan out to three times its original diameter. They were of a type once known as "Dum Dums" and quite illegal by every convention of war, peace or civilized behavior. They made the little Enfield a very horrible weapon.

As the train lurched over the bridge and came to a bellowing halt in the station, he finished his drink and laying a note beside his bill, shouldered his way out of the carriage and along the platform. The clock over the booking-office showed twenty minutes past eleven. "Red Knight" had done very well to make up those all important five minutes.

Kirk stood outside the barrier and looked around for Michael and Penny. He scowled as he waited for there were two things in life he loathed. One was being delayed and the other being cold; at the moment he was both. As he stood there, his frown suddenly turned to black fury as he found himself being examined by a grossly fat man with a piggy grin, railway uniform and quite incongruously, brown suede shoes.

"Yerse, you seem to be the fellow I'm after. Name of Kirk, isn't it?" The fat man came closer and peered at him. He had recently dined well and Kirk drew back before the blast of kippers.

"Yes, Kirk happens to be my name and what the devil is it to you?"

"Nothing to do with me, guv, nothing at all, thank goodness, but I've got something for you." He reached in the depths of his bulging jacket and brought out a crumpled sheet of paper. Even in the dim light of the badly lit station, Kirk recognized Michael's sprawling handwriting. He glanced briefly at it and then turned to his companion.

"Thank you," he said. "Now, my friend says that he has left a briefcase for me; just where have you got it?"

"I left it in the office, guv. Right across the hall over there. I didn't want to lug it across in case any questions were asked. Wouldn't be at all the thing for a man in my position to be seen carrying passengers' luggage about would it? Besides—" He broke off under Kirk's malevolent glance and meekly led the way across the hall to his post.

The room was pleasantly warm with a fire glowing in the grate and a kettle on the hob; Michael's case was on a deal table beside the telephone. The man lifted it down with a gesture that made it seem incredibly heavy and burdensome and handed it to Kirk. His voice became lower and more confidential.

"'Ere we are, sir, all safe and sound, just as I promised. I shouldn't really have left the office to meet you, but seeing your friend said it was urgent and he seemed such a pleasant gentleman, I took a big chance on it. By the way, your friend said you would be sure to see I was all right, sir."

"Did he, indeed? That was most kind and thoughtful of my friend. Yes, I'll see that you are all right, as you say. As a matter of fact the head controller for this area is a very old friend of mine. Yes, that's quite correct, Sir William Bevis. In return for your kindness, I will be sure to say nothing to him about your infringement of the rules.

"Now, just poke up your fire, put a chair in front of it and make me a cup of tea."

"A cup of tea—for passengers—in this office!" The man prepared himself for an outraged protest but something in Kirk's friendly smile cut him short. There was a shadow of the leering face of Sir William Bevis in that smile. Almost at once his protest died to cringing subservience.

"Of course, sir—a very great pleasure—right away, sir. Charlie, get moving; draw up a chair for this gentleman and start making the tea." He bawled at his assistant and plunged a poker into the already glowing fire. "Anything more I can do for you, sir?"

"Nothing, for the moment, thank you, except to keep out of my way and stop breathing down my neck." Kirk settled himself down by the fire and rubbed his hands before it. Then he lit a cigar and once more read through the note that Michael had left him.

It was quite clear and it was a trap; it had to be. As he looked at Michael's description of Penny's voice, with its jerky, automatic, strained quality, he saw that at once. Michael had not gone to meet her because he felt she had discovered something, but because he knew that something had discovered her. He had not gone through any sense of duty but purely because he was frightened for her safety. Kirk didn't blame him in the slightest, but as he looked at the writing, a frown crossed his face and he was very worried.

If Penny had been threatened and forced to phone Michael, it meant that his opponents were far in front of him and gaining.

They must have known every move he had made and every question he had asked. And it was his own fault, for he had completely failed to realize the thing he was up against. Now he would have to be careful and there would be no chance of dashing in through the front door. The front door would be blocked and he would have to find a way round.

"Thank you." He took the mug of tea from Charlie and started to read through the papers in Michael's case. They were divided into two halves and the first dealt with the religious groups in the neighborhood. After a minute he pushed them away and took up the survey plan. There was nothing in the religious side that fitted, no tie-up of names or locality, they had been far too clever for that.

As he looked at the map, however, he stiffened. For it was there, just exactly where he had hoped to find it; the way in.

At the top of the flight of steps to the river there stood the tall disused house with the inscription over the door. The inscription which had been carved just after the French Revolution and tied up with everything he had heard about M'sieu Albert le Petit. And suppose that, before him, years before him, somebody else had seen that inscription and guessed its significance. Somebody who needed just that little bit of reassurance to change thought into action. If that was the truth, what other meeting place could that person choose?

He ran his finger down the plan and the rest of the puzzle began to fit together.

Every one of those houses had a big three-roomed cellar. They were cut deep down in the lime-stone of the valley and the main drains ran beside them. And much more than the drains. At the top of the bank there had once stood a factory. It had been torn down and demolished to make way for the foundations of the bridge, but some part of it remained. A long shaft, which must once have carried waste to the river, ran beneath the steps to the edge of the sump and it passed very close to the cellars of the tall house which was called "Petit Albert."

It was still marked on the plan and at its foot there was a red cross and a line of neat writing. "Deemed unsafe, and blocked off by an iron-mesh door. Orders of the Council June the twenty-second nineteen hundred and twelve."

An iron-mesh door? Well, so what. Even though they were rusted solid, there were still ways by which a very determined person could open doors; iron or otherwise.

He pushed back his chair and ignoring the frown of his companions reached for the phone. He was just about to dial the police and speak to Hailstone when his hand went back to his side. That wasn't the way it had to be because the front way would be blocked. It was barred. Just let him go blundering into that house with a bevy of police on his heels and Penny and Michael would die. They would die very horribly, he was sure of that. He turned away from the phone, closed Michael's case and smiled at the stout man.

"Thank you very much, both for your tea and your civility. There is just one more thing I want you to do for me and then I will leave you in peace. Have you got a sheet of paper and an envelope? Thank you."

He sat down at the table and scrawled a note which he sealed carefully and handed to him.

"I hope that I shall be back to collect my friend's case and suitably reward you for your pains by eight o'clock in the morning. If, for any reason, I don't turn up, I want you to take this to your local police station. You are to take it personally, but on no account are you to read it." His friendly tone altered slightly.

"On no account whatsoever. Is that clear?"

"Yes, sir, of course, sir, just as you say, sir." A long time ago, the fat man had been a sergeant in the Royal Northumberland Fusiliers and he recognized Kirk's tone. His sagging body seemed to stiffen and draw in a little.

"Thank you, till eight o'clock then." Without another word, Kirk turned on his heel and walked out of the door.

The rain had stopped as he came through the station entrance but the streets were wet and glistening and there was a damp salty tang in the air. He walked quickly down the street towards the river and turned right in the direction of the bridge. Behind him the cathedral clock began to strike midnight. He turned up his collar and put his hands in his pocket. The cold hardness of the little Enfield felt the most comforting thing in the world.

As he reached the rail of the bridge he stopped and leaned over, releasing the cigar from his lips and watching its tiny red glow as it spun through the damp air and vanished in the river far below. The water looked like a grey concrete line in the dim light with the quay-side on its left. In the distance he could just make out the back-water with a break beside it that was the foot of the river steps and on the opposite bank there was the same cluster of lights as a big freighter began to unload. It was another ship now, though. The "Rosa Luxemburg" would be nearly home, clawing her way through the Kattegat to the Baltic and she was completely unimportant. He cursed himself for his foolishness in believing she had ever been. As far as this story was concerned she might never have existed. He straightened from the rail and walked on.

The main left hand pillar of the bridge was hollow and it had an elevator shaft running down inside it. The elevator must have closed hours ago, but the gates at the top were open and there was a flight of stairs beside the shaft. Kirk walked down the steps with his feet ringing on the concrete and the little blue lights on the walls giving the place a weird and somehow unpleasant effect. Not too unpleasant for some people however. Halfway down, a courting couple drew shyly away from him as they pressed into a corner of the stairs. He raised his hat, grinned, and wished them a polite "good-evening."

The quay-side itself was lit by old-fashioned gas lights and it seemed completely deserted. There were large puddles on the cracked stone paving and from time to time he stumbled over mooring rings and railway lines. In the same pocket as the gun he had a powerful electric flashlight, but he didn't want to use it just yet, so he walked on very carefully and slowly, till he passed the end of the quay proper where it ran into a stone jetty. And at the end of the jetty was the sump pit.

It looked even worse than when he had seen it before. Then he had been with other people and his mind had been wrapped up in a purely mathematical problem which he had long since solved. Or rather it could not be solved. There was no chance of the murder being committed in the ways that the police or even Michael had suggested. There was only one way, and only he knew it. Since he knew that the murdered girl was not Gerda Raine, he had not the slightest doubt in his mind as to how it had been done or by whom. All he had to find now was from *where*. Just let him find the path which had brought the real victim to the sump pit and it would take him to the killers.

He shivered slightly in the damp air and it did not come entirely from the cold. All around him were pictures hanging over the still water. Pictures of two respectable men, for instance, who had passed by, just where he was standing with a little white terrier pulling on its lead. They had gone on up the stairs, just as they did every night, and they would see Carlton. Then the place would be deserted again for a time and at last, out of nowhere, had come something.

Around a bend of the river there came a beat of propellers and panting steam and a tug came towards him with black smoke pluming at its funnel. On the bridge he could see a man standing with a pipe in his mouth; the same man probably, who, five days ago had heard a splash and the sound of running feet; the two sounds which he had been intended to hear. Kirk stood quite still in the shadows and watched the boat as it churned its way home under the bridges. Then he turned towards the long slope of the hill.

The steps ran upwards, straight in front of him and there was a row of dark derelict buildings on the right. Towards the left he could see a ragged gap which disappeared into a wilderness of ash, fallen brickwork and rubble. He thought of the lay-out of Michael's map and began to walk towards the gap. It was perhaps a little more than twenty yards across and at the back there was a low wall holding back the pressure of the slope above. He gave a quick glance behind him and then switched off his flashlight and walked cautiously across the waste ground to the wall with his feet slipping and sinking into the soft refuse.

He found what he was looking for almost at once. In the centre of the wall, just beside a buttress, there was an opening. It was a little brick arch about four feet square and it was closed by a heavy iron lattice. He swept his torch over the bars and the rusted hinges and the lock and his doubts vanished and he knew he was right. That was the way they had come. In the beam of his torch he could see a film of oil clinging to the lock and there was a glint of bright metal round the hinge bearers.

He studied the lock for a moment and then took the folder of tools from his pocket and selected a long curved wire. It entered the wide old-fashioned key hole easily and very gently he began to force it against the mechanism. At the first pressure he felt it slip home and the tongue of the lock move back. He pulled open the door and looked at the gap. It took him five minutes to work his way through it but at last he was standing inside the old shaft. Then he pulled the door to behind him and moved forwards.

The passage had had brick walls and once a wooden floor but that had gone years ago. There was stuff under his feet that might have been wood but it was soft and rotten and gave way at each step. From down the shaft there came an odor of decay that reminded him of every ghost story, childhood terror or Gothic novel he had ever known. From time to time he sank up to his ankles in water and lurched against the side of the dripping walls. Then at last he turned a corner and saw that the passage became a drain with a shoot of water coming down it and a narrow row of steps at the side.

Kirk held his light well down and followed the steps, keeping close to the wall. They were cracked and covered with slime and here and there water ran over them. The drain was very steep now and it carried quite a fair-sized stream. He counted sixty steps and then came to a barrier where part of the roof had fallen in and the steps were choked with bricks and rubble.

He swept his torch over the pile of masonry and then gingerly lowered himself into the water. It was very cold and swept round his knees. He gripped the light with his mutilated hand and held on to the edge of the steps with the left. Then he began to work round the pile of masonry. He was almost past it when he stopped.

He stopped quite dead and for a moment he didn't even breathe. The light slipped from his fingers and dropped into the water. It didn't go out at once but slid down the slope with its beam glinting up through the water like an illumination in an aquarium tank. Kirk stood motionless on the side of the steps and watched it die, then he reached in his pocket and brought out a box of matches. He wiped his hand carefully before he struck one and he prayed as it began to flare.

Then he looked at the thing that had made him stop. It lay on the edge of the step and he was holding it. It didn't look human at all and might have been part of a set of rather unpleasant practical jokes. It was human though; a small hand with blue veins and as he moved the match higher he saw the rest of the body. Just beyond the pile of rubble, jammed in against the wall and half-covered by sacking, was the dead body of Mrs. Carlton and she seemed to be smiling at him in the flicker of the match.

CHAPTER SIXTEEN

The big room was lit by a single naked light bulb and it was long and low and narrow and room was the wrong word for it; it was like a cave. It had no windows or carpet and the only furniture was a row of wooden chairs. The walls were of dark brick and here and there a little rivulet of water ran down them to the flagstone floor. It was the cellar beneath the big house at the top of the stairs and the meeting place of Little Albert.

Penny Wise sat quite still on her bent-wood chair and she looked straight in front of her, the chain had been removed when they had brought her in from the other room and she was free to move. She didn't move an inch. She kept her head fixed in front of her looking at the end of the room and she never looked sideways. On either side and behind her were the faces.

There were perhaps twenty people in the room and they stood along the walls behind her and they seemed to be waiting. They were of every size, age and appearance and the majority of them were women.

Penny had recognized some of them when Mrs. Brett had brought her in from the other room, but they had been different then. They had seemed very friendly then and one or two had even smiled at her. They had been like members of a women's institute welcoming a stranger to the whist-drive.

Now they had changed and Penny couldn't even look at their faces. She just kept her eyes fixed in front of her, looking towards the far end of the room while all around her came their soft breathing. At the end of the room there was Michael Howard.

Michael sat on the floor with his back to the brick wall and his eyes were closed. He breathed deeply and from time to time a little moan came from his open mouth. He was quite unconscious and when he had crawled into the room it had been a purely reflex action. Now the drug held him completely and he knew nothing.

Without raising her head Penny looked past Michael at the thing above him. It hung from the ceiling by thin wires and its polished wood shone in the light. It was the same figure as the carving in the next room, but much larger and the workmanship was purely European. In the harsh light, every repulsive detail of the dead eyes and bent limbs was clear to her and its shadow lay over the wall behind it like a cross. Just below it and to the right of Michael, screened partially by the shadow, there was an open doorway with a flight of steps leading down.

"This is just a dream, my dear. Please try and think of it as just a dream."

Mrs. Brett stood beside her and she stroked Penny's hand. Her voice was low and oddly comforting. As Penny felt her soft fingers running over her hand she knew that the woman hated what she had to do. She would still do it, however. Because of the thing on the wall she had to do it and in her own horrible way she was a saint.

"You see, my dear, it isn't us," she said. "We have nothing against you and we don't want to hurt you at all. We have to do it because it is the will of something far greater than ourselves. In your case I am very sorry, Mrs. Wise. I have a feeling about you, you see. I feel that you have been injured the way we have." She raised her hand and tilted Penny's head towards her.

"You had a husband, didn't you? Did he leave you for someone else?"

Penny looked at Mrs. Brett's cool smiling face and behind it she could see the woman with the birthmark. She was smiling too, but her smile was quite different. There was no sadness in her eyes, only expectation.

"No," she said, "he didn't leave me for anyone else, only for a bottle. Does that qualify me for a membership card to your menagerie? Now, just stop the loving-sister act and get on with it. Tell me where we are and what you are going to do to us."

"You are going to be seen, Mrs. Wise, that is all. As I told you, there is only one person we fear and that is General Kirk. Therefore he is in our way and we are going to destroy him. You and Mr. Howard are to be our tools." The fingers left her face and once more played across her hand.

"The time is just after midnight. By now General Kirk will have given up waiting for you at the station and gone either to the police or to his hotel. In either case there will be a message waiting for him. It will be from you and Mr. Howard and will be full of apologies for keeping him waiting. It will ask him to meet you at the foot of the river steps at half past eleven. I am rather good at reading character and I am quite sure that Kirk will come alone without a police escort. Do you understand me now, Mrs. Wise?"

"Yes, now I begin to understand." Penny turned away from that smiling face and tried to think.

It would be the same way as before. The substitution of Gerda Raine for somebody else. And this time the somebody would be herself. Gerda Raine was now Penny Wise. Her mind was gone but she was still quite capable of obeying orders. Penny looked down at her clothes; while she was under the drug they had changed them. She was wearing a costume which should have been in her wardrobe at the hotel and just to the right of Mrs. Brett she could see a figure standing by the wall who wore the dress she had had on that evening.

"Good, it will be quite simple. As simple as it was the other time. You now have two selves, Mrs. Wise, and while you were here your other self has been working very hard for us. *You* were taken out of 'Cherry's' by the back door, but *she* came back into the dance hall in your clothes and, because she seemed a little the worse for drink, my son took her to the hotel.

"When they got there, she went up to your room for a while and then came down and handed a note typed on your machine to the clerk. It was to be given to General Kirk as soon as he returned. When people are a little intoxicated they tend to look different and I think the clerk was able to recognize you without much difficulty.

"After that, your other self made a telephone call. Yes, that's right, to the police, leaving the message for Kirk. She didn't really make it of course, because that's too difficult for her; but I did and the time that she was in the box and the time of the message are the same. Exactly ten fifteen." She glanced at her watch as she said it.

"And then?" Penny's question was purely rhetorical; she already knew the rest of the plan. It was quite simple and very efficient. As far as anybody would know, Kirk would come to the meeting place at her request. She alone would appear the prime-mover.

"And then we waited a little, but now it is time to start. By now General Kirk will be on his way. He will go to the river steps and he will be expecting to meet you and Mr. Howard. We will see that he is not disappointed.

"Just past the sump pit to the right of the steps there is a piece of waste land and Mr. Howard will be waiting for him there. He will be quite dead and there will be a knife wound in his back.

"I want you to listen very carefully now because it is the crux of the story and I am rather proud of it.

"Kirk will find Mr. Howard's body at exactly twelve thirty and at twelve thirty-two there is a police patrol passing. They have had that patrol there since the first murder and it is always on time. You can almost set your watch by them.

"When Kirk sees the body he will bend down and look at it and that will be the last thing he does, because you, Mrs. Wise, your other self will be ready and waiting for him with the same knife that killed Mr. Howard."

"Don't go on, I understand." Penny stared straight ahead at Michael and she felt cold and helpless and quite numb. If ten policemen waving batons had suddenly appeared at the opening in the wall she wouldn't have been able to cry out to them.

Beyond Michael, beyond the shadow of the foul thing on the wall, beyond the cellar and through the rock that stretched to the river she could picture the end of the story. She could see Kirk bending down over the body and at the same instance a creature that looked like her and wore her dress coming out of the shadows with its knife. She saw the police rounding the bend and seeing the knife as it went home and following her other self. Following it up the stairs till they came to the top and then they would find her. They would find the real Penny Wise lying in front of them, dead, but still warm, with the knife beside her, while in front of her Gerda Raine would run on towards the main road and the person who was waiting to meet her.

It would work, of course; they would put it down as temporary insanity brought on by the horror of the last few days. Through some pent-up emotion she would have killed Michael and when Kirk had found her out she had taken the knife and added the second murder. It would all be kept very quiet. The department did not like publicity and her suicide would be readily accepted by Kirk's successor. She forced herself to look round at the faces behind her and as she watched their set, purposeful expressions she felt cold and paralyzed and without hope. Very faint and far away through the flagged ceiling, the cathedral clock struck one note.

"Quarter past twelve, it is time now." Mrs. Brett left her side and walked towards Michael. She tilted his face towards the light and looked at his closed eyes. For about half a minute she looked at him, then she laid the head slightly sideways so that the throat was in the full beam of the light. Then she turned and spoke partly to Penny and partly to the rest of the people in the room.

"Now, I shall answer your first question, my dear. 'Where are we?'" All the mildness went out of her face suddenly and she looked quite different.

"You are in the house of our faith. Long ago when I was in my agony I saw this house and I read the words over the door. I knew at once what those words meant, because I had seen them before when I was abroad. I knew then that I had been chosen to bring my faith to this country and tell others about it.

"There were once two men, Mrs. Wise, who were persecuted and driven from their country. One came here and lived in this house. He was a follower of the thing that we follow, but because the time was not ripe, he died, and his knowledge died with him. All that was left was the inscription over the door of his house. The other man went farther away and there his wisdom grew till it became a power and later I found it.

"This house has become our meeting place and in it we have put our symbol. Look at that symbol, Mrs. Wise. Look at the face of our god."

Penny looked up at the carving and all at once it started to grow. The wood of the face shone as with a light of its own and its shadow was monstrous behind it. It was just a trick, an illusion, the effect of a lamp that somebody had switched on from the back of the room, but to Penny it was terror. As she looked at that blind face in front of her she realized why Mrs. Brett's words had sounded so quiet and automatic. They were just words she was told to say: they didn't come from her at all but from something outside herself which was the real director.

"Kneel," she said. "It is time for you to kneel because very soon the matter will be finished; so kneel before the thing you are about to die for." As the light swept across her face, Penny saw that the woman was weeping.

Then there were hands on her shoulders forcing her forward and she was on her knees on the stone floor while another hand held her head so that it was pointing up at the carving. All around her she heard a scraping of chairs and cloth as the other women went down on the floor before "Little Albert."

"Yes, it is time. Does everybody know what they have to do?

You—and you—and you." Mrs. Brett looked at the people in front of her and one by one they answered her with a simple affirmative. They were as organized as a troop of soldiers before action, or servers at the Mass.

"Good. In two minutes, we will start. First though, let us look at the thing which we follow."

She bent down and placed something in front of the carving and almost at once the room became filled with the smell of camphor and the figure seemed to grow larger.

In spite of her horror, Penny kept her eyes fixed on it and it moved. It swayed in front of her and it swelled outwards till it was the only living thing in the room. There was nothing that anybody in the world could do to stop the advance of that crippled blind god.

"Come here." The woman with the thin mouth who was called Mrs. Travers got up from her knees and walked forward. She stopped in front of Gerda Raine and smiled at her.

"Take it," she said and brought something out of the sleeve of her coat. It glinted slightly in the staring light.

"Take it," she said, "take it and use it, now."

The imbecile looked at the knife for a moment and she didn't seem to know what it was. She just stood quite still and watched it and then her hand reached out and felt the blade. Rather horribly she giggled. Then, like a well-oiled machine, her fingers spread and grasped the hilt and she balanced it in her hand. As soon as she was sure she had got the feel and balance of it she moved towards Michael.

Penny screamed. For a long time fear had held her like the remains of the drug, but with the glint of the steel it slipped away and she became a purely wild and primitive creature fighting for the thing she loved. She hurled herself forward from the chair and a moment later she had Gerda Raine in her arms.

And even in her fury she kept her head. It wasn't conscious, it wasn't thought out at all, but she knew what she had to do. It was as if there was a voice behind her telling her exactly what she had to do. She paid no attention to the arms that were around her body pulling her backwards or the knife that was swinging down on her, and concentrated on the one thing that might save Michael. She took Gerda's right arm between her arms, twisted her body till it was pressing like a lever against the fulcrum of the elbow and slipped forward. Then she stood up and allowed herself to be led quietly back to her chair.

"You fool, you wretched, interfering, foolish fool." Mrs. Brett stood in front of her and at each adjective, her hand came down across Penny's face.

And Penny didn't care. She hardly felt the blows at all. She just looked forward towards Gerda Raine and she had never felt better in her life, because she had won.

The girl stood silent in the lamp-light and she didn't look as if she was hurt at all. There was not a trace of expression in her face and everything might have been as it was before.

But everything wasn't. The knife lay on the flag-stones at her feet and her right hand hung at her side limp and useless. Penny had made no mistake. Her pressure and her timing had been quite correct. The arm was broken and Mrs. Brett would have to find another killer.

"Stop it, that will do us no good." The woman beside Gerda stepped forward and pulled Mrs. Brett back. "There is not time for reprisals, now, but we can still win, because we have something to fight for.

"You, Mrs. Wise, may think you are clever because you have broken an arm, but that will not help you. She still has feet, you see, and she can still run when the policemen find her."

She moved back to Gerda Raine and lifted her arm. It was discolored and lay quite limp in her hand but there was no flicker of pain in Gerda's face.

"Yes, she can still run and it is time for us to stop playing and begin. Is everything else ready?" She looked at the women behind Penny and then picked up the knife.

"Very well, we shall go on as though nothing had happened. Our little friend here has lost the use of her arm, but that need not stop us. I will be her arm. There is plenty of cover beside the sump and all the police will see will be a woman killing and a woman running. We will start, now."

She stroked the blade of the knife and then moved towards Michael. She smiled as she moved and Penny saw that if Mrs. Brett was a saint who acted as her god told her, this woman loved what she was going to do. She felt the hands on her body holding her back and knew that all further resistance was useless. Then she closed her eyes and waited for the end.

It never came. Just as Mrs. Travers raised her hand and the knife drew back there was a noise. It was quite faint and didn't sound like anything at all and it came from the stairs behind her.

"Wait." The woman with the birthmark spoke hoarsely behind Penny's back. Even with the gag they had forced over her nose and mouth, Penny smelled the wine fumes on her breath.

"Wait and listen; something is coming."

If it were possible, the already quiet room became still more silent. But the sound stopped. There was nothing to be heard, nothing at all except the soft breathing. Mrs. Brett looked up at her from beside the statue.

"Nobody is coming, sister, nobody at all. It was just water on the stone that you heard and nobody can come up. No one but ourselves knows the secret of the stairs." She motioned to Mrs. Travers and once more the knife rose in front of Michael and once more faltered.

For something *was* coming. Something was coming up the stairs behind them and it was getting louder as it came. The soft noise had turned to footsteps now and they were coming quickly.

The women who were holding Penny let go her arms and stared ahead of them quite motionless. From far away down the passage, beyond the sound came the distant wail of a ship's siren. Mrs. Brett walked forward and stood in front of the carving.

"Nobody can come up those steps; nobody else knows about them. Nobody human, that is. But I think I know what is coming. It is he and he is coming here to give us his blessing." She dropped down on her knees and looked at the doorway with her face glowing with love, adoration and mania.

And the thing was very close now. The thud of its feet on the stairs was loud and heavy and all at once and rather horribly it started to sing. Even in her terror, Penny could distinguish the words. They were in Latin and the voice was flat and completely tuneless.

"Alberti Minimi Sacris Laus et Gloria Magistri," sang the flat voice and the doorway began to darken. Then, into the room, came "Little Albert."

"Little Albert" stood back in the shadow of his image and he was horrible. His face was half in darkness, but his body was dripping. Water streamed from it and formed little pools on the stone floor of the cellar. A musty smell came from his body and there was green slime on the rags that covered him. He stepped forward into the light and something at his side glinted.

"Ladies, ladies, dear sweet, lovely ladies," said General Kirk and the gun in his hand came up quickly.

CHAPTER SEVENTEEN

They had turned off the lights and it was already quite late in the morning when at last Hailstone pushed back his chair and drained the dregs of his coffee. He looked round the room at Penny and Michael and Inspector Ellis and grinned at Kirk. Under the grin his face was a mixture of three expressions, irritation, bewilderment and faint now but beginning pleasure at the thought of a job completed.

"Well, General, I suppose you could put me down as satisfied but not entirely convinced," he said. "It must have been as you say, but my word, she was clever about it, wasn't she? The way she must have watched and studied each of those women before she put her proposition to them."

"I doubt it, Captain Hailstone, I don't for one moment believe that that would have been necessary." Kirk still wore the suit in which he had crawled up the tunnel and the mud had dried on it, giving him a stiff and unnatural appearance like a cinema monster.

"People do recognize each other, you know. Masons have signs for instance and I have read in many books that the most out of the way sexual perverts are able to see each other's tastes at a glance. I think her contacts must have come quite automatically."

"Yes, but the way she brought them together; the organization was fantastic. The whole thing sounds more like one of Grimm's grimmer fairy stories than real life."

"I suppose it does, old boy. Not Grimm though, much earlier and much more basic in every way. Cinderella perhaps. Yes, I fancy Cinderella, but with a difference. In this case it was the ugly sisters who felt ill-treated and found the fairy godmother." He got up from his chair, ground out the stump of his cigar into an ash tray that was shaped like a cricket ball and crossed to the window. The sun was quite high over the town now and in the street below a grey, cloth-capped army were hurrying to work.

"Yes, the ugly sisters, the slighted sisters, the ones that nobody really wanted. The women who had all lost their love when Cinderella came along with her little glass slippers. Gerda Raine, Cinderella, or a hundred other girls. What's in a name?

"There must be lots of ugly sisters in the world you know. Women who have lost something and cling to the last bit of love left which is usually a child. And when that is taken go sour."

"Yes, I daresay you're right." Hailstone snorted and began to fiddle with his empty pipe.

"Still, they don't as a rule band themselves together into a murder organization, do they?"

"No, mercifully they don't as a rule. In the first place they never get the opportunity and there is a social conscience there to check them. They may have their wishes, however, their day-dreams, just below the surface." He looked round at Hailstone and his hand drummed quietly on the glass of the window.

"In this case, just like the fairy story you mentioned, it seems that their wishes were granted and dreams became reality.

"In this case they found the fairy godmother, Mrs. Brett, who was able to give them everything they wanted. I think Mrs. Brett was a near-genius in her own way and she must have been a great hater even before her marriage broke up. When she was in Madagascar she came in contact with a story that confirmed all her personal hate; 'Petit Albert' and the legend of Queen Ranavalo.

"Then she came home to this city and quite by chance saw the house with the inscription. I think that must have unhinged her and made her actions seem dedicated. As we know now and should have checked before, the lease of the house was taken over by her and put in the name of her first convert, Mrs. Travers.

"The rest is easy to follow. Being a woman of great strength and purpose, she spread her message, her religion if you like, among others and very soon there was an organization. It was probably quite harmless at first, no different from any other lunatic sect, till she had her second injury; the death of her brother at the hands of Gerda Raine. After that they went into action.

"By some means that we'll probably never know, Gerda Raine was traced and brought up here. The idea was never to kill her, but to destroy her and they did that very effectively. Then something went wrong. Mrs. Travers' maid found out what they were doing and tried a little blackmail. She had to die, of course, and because they saw her resemblance to Gerda they decided on a very novel method. Carlton was made the scapegoat and then cleared by the testimony of two quite impeccable witnesses. That's the lot, I think. They only needed to get myself out of the way, bury Mrs. Carlton in the tunnel and everything would have gone on as before."

"Yes, I suppose you're right and we missed it." Hailstone rapped his pipe on the desk and scowled at Ellis. "I'm afraid I can't compliment you, Inspector, on the way this case has been handled."

"Easy on, old boy." Kirk walked back to his chair and picked up his coat.

"There's nobody to blame and I deserve no credit. I got on the scent purely by chance. I saw the carving in the maid's room and it rang a bell. It reminded me of something a fool of a missionary had once told me during my unhappy school days. After that I just followed my hunch, completely blind. It was only when I heard that the murdered girl was not Gerda Raine that I began to see daylight. If anybody deserves a kick in the pants, I do. I blundered in on that doctor woman like the greenest amateur. Another five minutes coming up that tunnel and there would have quite literally been the devil to pay."

"Yes, you're right, General, nobody is to blame. Still it's been a horrible business and it will take a lot of explanation to the Home Secretary. Twenty-three women and all insane; twenty-five if you count the two you had to kill in the cellar."

"Hardly insane, Captain Hailstone; merely possessed, I think. Believe me, there is a difference. I feel that at the beginning this business started out as a mere game, a mere ritual and then it got out of hand and they honestly began to think they were the chosen servants of a god. The terrible thing is that it wouldn't have stopped with just a few deaths. Even if they had got away with killing Mrs. Wise, Mr. Howard and myself, it wouldn't have stopped. I think that from time to time that blind god would have demanded a few more sacrifices." Kirk put on his coat and buttoned it tightly. Then he wound a woolen scarf round his neck and held out his hand to Hailstone.

"Well, goodbye, Chief Constable. You've still got a lot of details that need clearing up, but it shouldn't be too difficult I fancy. Now that their leader is dead, those women will talk all right. I'm sorry I had to shoot her and Mrs. Travers of course, but Mr. Howard was on the point of getting a knife across his throat and I value his life, though he has been a bloody fool as far as this business is concerned.

"Gerda Raine will go soon, I suppose. Yes, the doctor told me he gave her two or three days at the outside and I have no doubt it is the best thing that can happen.

"Well, goodbye once more and I'm glad to have been of some service, though I can't compliment myself on the way this business has been managed. Coming, children?"

He motioned to Michael and Penny to follow him, nodded to Ellis and walked out of the door. When it had shut behind them he stopped and grinned.

"Well, that's that. We've broken it, the three of us, just as we said we would. Left those silly bleeders with a packet of work to clear up and it won't give them a scrap of glory, either. They'll never take them to court. All they'll get will be a large influx of patients in the local asylums. And that reminds me." The grin died on his face and he rounded on them like a blight.

"Now for your future guidance, I've got a couple of things to say to the two of you, and I'm extremely annoyed at the way you've behaved.

"In the future, you, Penny, will grow up and look before you drink, while you, Mike, had better learn to use a little common-sense and keep your emotions to yourself. You may have been shaken up by having to kill Mrs. Carlton, but that is no excuse for acting like Little Lord—What was the fellow's name? Thank you, Fauntleroy. If, in the future, anyone threatens to spray you with acid, shoot first and kiss afterwards is better.

"Now, let's stop chattering here and get back to the hotel. As soon as we've packed our things we're taking the next train back to London."

"To London, General Kirk? But what about the rest of your holiday; aren't you going back to the grouse-shooting?" Penny's surprise was quite false and came as a reprisal for his reprimand. She winked at Michael as she said it and then froze before Kirk's scowl.

"No, Mrs. Wise, I am not going back for the grouse-shooting; I am not able to. The incompetence of my inferiors has rendered that quite impossible, I'm afraid. As I said, I am returning to London, where I intend to run my department in the efficient way I am accustomed to. Now, let's get going."

He strode forward to the door of the police station, nodded to the constable who opened it for him and began to walk down the stairs. On the third step from the bottom he stopped.

He stopped dead as though he had seen a ghost or had a sudden heart attack and he stood quite still with his jaw hanging open. His breath came in jerks and his face was flushed as he looked at the thing in front of him.

The Rolls-Royce was of an early vintage and covered with

mud. It had a tartan fabric body, much the worse for wear, and an enormous open boot. The driver had a uniform cap over his receding forehead and chin, but he didn't look a proper chauffeur. He grinned at Kirk, made a pretence of touching his cap and then pulled open the back door.

A horrible man got out. He was bow-legged, purple-faced and wore loud plus-fours, a deer stalker hat with a feather in it and very thick brogues. He beamed at Kirk and hurried across the pavement shouting as he came.

"Ah, there you are, old chap—thought I'd find you here—just in time to meet you, eh." Fetherstone Clumber-Holt's hand came down on Kirk's shoulder like a piston.

"Lucky catching you, but that feller Hailstone is a pal of mine and he told me you were here." He half pulled, half pushed him down the steps towards the Rolls.

"You've finished here now, haven't you? Good show; hope the chap you were after gets his deserts. Glossop has already collected your togs from the hotel, so we can get straight off.

"Good morning, Howard. Can you manage to join us? Pity, but don't apologize, we'll see you sometime I expect. Mustn't stop now as it's already gone nine and we have to be on the moors by ten. No, no, in you get, old chap." He cut short Kirk's feeble protests and forced him into the car. Just before he climbed in himself, he turned and shouted to Michael.

"I've kept my promise, Howard. Going to give the general the time of his life. Just as I said I would, I've saved 'Wet Hollow' for him."

Michael and Penny stood quite still at the top of the steps and they both felt utterly helpless with dismay and with a nearly insuperable desire to burst out laughing. Penny took Michael's hand and moved closer to him as they watched the big car turn slowly round and begin to move down the street.

John Blackburn (1923-1993)
Photo by Laura Richardson, Weston, Mass.
(From the dust jacket of the 1962 American edition of *Broken Boy*)

ALSO AVAILABLE FROM VALANCOURT BOOKS

Michael Arlen	Hell! said the Duchess
R. C. Ashby (Ruby Ferguson)	He Arrived at Dusk
Frank Baker	The Birds
Charles Beaumont	The Hunger and Other Stories
David Benedictus	The Fourth of June
Charles Birkin	The Smell of Evil
John Blackburn	A Scent of New-Mown Hay
	Broken Boy
	Blue Octavo
	The Flame and the Wind
	Nothing but the Night
	Bury Him Darkly
	The Household Traitors
	Our Lady of Pain
	The Face of the Lion
	The Cyclops Goblet
	A Beastly Business
	The Bad Penny
Thomas Blackburn	The Feast of the Wolf
John Braine	Room at the Top
	The Vodi
Jack Cady	The Well
R. Chetwynd-Hayes	The Monster Club
Basil Copper	The Great White Space
	Necropolis
Hunter Davies	Body Charge
Jennifer Dawson	The Ha-Ha
Frank De Felitta	The Entity
Barry England	Figures in a Landscape
Ronald Fraser	Flower Phantoms
Gillian Freeman	The Liberty Man
	The Leather Boys
	The Leader
Stephen Gilbert	The Landslide
	Bombardier
	Monkeyface
	The Burnaby Experiments
	Ratman's Notebooks

Martyn Goff	The Plaster Fabric
	The Youngest Director
	Indecent Assault
Stephen Gregory	The Cormorant
Thomas Hinde	Mr. Nicholas
	The Day the Call Came
Claude Houghton	I Am Jonathan Scrivener
	This Was Ivor Trent
Gerald Kersh	Nightshade and Damnations
	Fowlers End
	Night and the City
Francis King	To the Dark Tower
	Never Again
	An Air That Kills
	The Dividing Stream
	The Dark Glasses
	The Man on the Rock
C.H.B. Kitchin	Ten Pollitt Place
	The Book of Life
Hilda Lewis	The Witch and the Priest
John Lodwick	Brother Death
Kenneth Martin	Aubade
	Waiting for the Sky to Fall
Michael Nelson	Knock or Ring
	A Room in Chelsea Square
Beverley Nichols	Crazy Pavements
Oliver Onions	The Hand of Kornelius Voyt
Robert Phelps	Heroes and Orators
J.B. Priestley	Benighted
	The Doomsday Men
	The Other Place
	The Magicians
	The Shapes of Sleep
	Saturn Over the Water
	The Thirty-First of June
	Salt is Leaving
Peter Prince	Play Things
Piers Paul Read	Monk Dawson
Forrest Reid	The Garden God
	Following Darkness

Lightning Source UK Ltd.
Milton Keynes UK
UKHW01f2109240918
329455UK00001B/317/P